How NOT To Survive A Zombie Apocalypse

Jinx Blade

Published by Blade & Co, 2024.

HOW NOT TO SURVIVE A ZOMBIE APOCALYPSE

First edition. May 16, 2024.

Copyright © 2024 Jinx Blade.

ISBN: 979-8224524532

Written by Jinx Blade.

Table of Contents

Zombie Movie Quotes:
Zombie TV Shows with Quotes

Introduction

Welcome to the absurd world of a zombie apocalypse. Where survival instincts face the ultimate test against the undead, revealing hilariously ridiculous demises of characters.

In these pages, discover fifty-one tales of doom, from the reckless, dimwitted to the foolish.

Each story showcases humanity's knack for fatally stupid decisions in the face of danger.

And that's not all! Dive into interactive trivia, deliberately bad surviving tips, poems, jokes, and beloved movie and TV quotes for some lighthearted fun.

So grab your puke bucket, lace up your shoes, gather your loved ones, and brace yourself for a journey through the silliest—and most entertaining—doomsday scenarios ever.

Chapter 1

Jack the Elevator Enthusiast had always marveled at the ingenious invention that allowed people to move effortlessly between floors. His passion for vertical transportation bordered on obsession. His knowledge of their inner workings rivaled that of more seasoned engineers. He spent countless hours studying elevator designs, memorizing every detail of their mechanisms, and he even had a collection of themed memorabilia that adorned his apartment.

He had received a call to investigate a possible malfunction in an elevator in a high-rise building. Busy with other jobs at the time, he had put it last on his to-do list. When he arrived at the towering complex, he rode the elevator to the top floor and his ears picked up the fault straight away. Recognizing it as an issue with the braking mechanism, he was about to seal it off and head down the fire exit to start fixing it. But then, without warning, zombies appeared.

The sight of the flesh-eaters impacted his cognitive abilities, leaving him undecided whether to take the stairs or the faulty elevator. As the undead drew closer, he opted for the fastest way to escape, in spite of the warnings going off in his head. Setting aside his vast knowledge of elevators, he rushed back to the lift, stepped inside, and pressed the button for ground level.

While he prayed that the brakes wouldn't falter on the way down, the doors closed and the elevator began its descent. Two levels down, it screeched to a halt when the power died, leaving him suspended between floors in the claustrophobic confines of a metal cage. As darkness enveloped him and panic set in, he fumbled for the emergency button, only to realize it was as lifeless as the elevator itself during an electrical outage.

With a groan of frustration, his eyes darted to the hatch in the ceiling above, now his only means of escape. Summoning his inner kangaroo, he bounded upward with all the grace of a spring-loaded toy, his arms waving like windmill blades in a hurricane. However, his fingertips barely grazed the latch as he reached for it.

Undeterred, he attempted to scale the walls like a demented spider. But his feet slid off the smooth surface like an ice skater on a frozen lake, and he landed squarely on his ass with an undignified thud.

As the severity of his predicament sank in, Jack plopped down on the floor. Contemplating his dire situation while frustration bubbled in his mind like a pimple ripe with pus, his thoughts raced a mile a minute. Each passing moment adding to his growing sense of unease.

Distressed, he repeatedly tried to jump up again, each failed attempt causing the elevator car to sway ominously. As he frantically struggled, noises from the shaft finally reached his ears. He knew the grinding and screeching meant one thing—the brakes were about to give out. The eerie sounds sent shivers across his neck, amplifying his perception of impending danger. All at once, the car began to plummet, descending ten floors with a stomach-churning drop that left Jack's heart lodged in his throat as he braced for impact.

The abrupt stop jolted him about like the sudden snip of a puppet's strings. Flung to the floor with a loud bang, he found it momentarily impossible to catch his breath. With quivering hands, he tried to pry open the doors. But they remained stubbornly sealed, mocking his feeble attempts at escape.

Panic set in as he realized he was trapped in this metal coffin. Despite his encyclopedic knowledge of elevator mechanics, he found himself unable to resolve the situation. Frustration bubbled up inside him again, and he began to leap up and down once more in a fruitless attempt to access the latch, again causing the elevator to sway.

His frenzied movements sent Jack plummeting another five floors, the elevator's descent a chaotic whirlwind of terror. As he grasped for any semblance of control, his mind raced with anxiety. Then, with newfound resolve, he focused his energy on prying the stubborn doors open.

This time, they creaked reluctantly apart—only to present him with a ghastly sight. A decomposing hand, its flesh mottled with shades of sickly green and gray, emerged from behind the opening. The putrid odor of rot wafted into the cramped space, assaulting Jack's senses with its foul stench.

The hand's skin was peeling and blistered, revealing patches of exposed muscle and bone beneath. Short, yellowed fingernails, cracked and jagged, protruded from gnarled fingertips like misshapen talons. Slimy tendrils of ichor oozed from the decaying tissue, leaving a trail of viscous slime in their wake.

With sickening squelches, the hand groped blindly, its movements jerky and erratic as it reached for anything nearby with urgent, grasping motions. Jack recoiled in horror, his heart pounding in his chest as he fought the urge to retch at the gruesome spectacle before him.

Pulling himself together, he pushed the doors shut, severing the hand from its decomposing owner. But to his shock, the detached hand continued to twitch and crawl across the floor, its fingers flexing and curling like tiny legs.

With a mixture of disgust and terror, he leapt onto the walls of the elevator car, only to slide off as he tried to dodge the alarming advance of the animated appendage. In a desperate bid to get rid of the undead hand, he stomped on it with all his might, expecting that to do the trick. Yet, to his dismay, it refused to stay down.

With mounting shock and horror, he watched it scurry across the floor, grab hold of his pants, and begin rapidly climbing up toward his throat. With shudders of revulsion, he engaged in a frenetic game of tug-of-war, pulling it off his body only for it to keep returning with renewed vigor.

In a last-ditch effort to fend off the unrelenting hand, he shoved it into his jacket pocket and zipped it up, hoping to contain its determined assault. With the ghoulish appendage safely stowed away, he resumed his frantic jumping, his movements fueled by a dire urge to get out of his steel prison.

His hysterical bouncing dislodged the brakes again, and the elevator descended with a resounding bang. The sound echoed in the metal cage, its reverberations echoing through the enclosure like a thunderclap in a confined space. With each gut-wrenching lurch downward, his stomach churned with nauseating dread.

As the car hurtled toward the ground, the sound of the air filling with grinding gears was punctuated by the panicked beating of his heart. With a final, bone-rattling impact, it slammed into the ground at bottom of the elevator shaft, the effect of the collision sending shockwaves rippling through Jack's body like a violent earthquake. The doors, weakened by the crash, buckled under the strain, blowing outward with explosive force to leave a ragged, gaping hole in their wake.

By sheer miracle, he emerged unscathed. Dusting himself off, he staggered through the opening. Then a roaming group of zombies charged at him with bloodcurdling, hungry moans. With a nervous gulp, he helplessly accepted his fate.

Zombie Movie & TV Trivia: Round 1

1. In George A. Romero's classic *Night of the Living Dead*, where does the zombie outbreak begin?
2. What is the name of the virus that causes the zombie apocalypse in *28 Days Later*?
3. Which actor played the lead role in *World War Z*, a film based on Max Brooks' novel of the same name?
4. In *Shaun of the Dead*, what item does Shaun use to fight off zombies in the pub?
5. What is the iconic rule #1 that Columbus follows in *Zombieland*?
6. In *Dawn of the Dead* (2004), survivors take refuge in a shopping mall. Where is the original 1978 version set?
7. Which 2009 zombie comedy film features Jesse Eisenberg and Woody Harrelson as unlikely allies in a post-apocalyptic world?
8. What is the name of the security operative team sent to investigate The Hive in *Resident Evil*?
9. Who directed the 2016 South Korean zombie film *Train to Busan*?
10. In *Warm Bodies*, what unusual trait does the zombie named "R" possess?

Answers will be found after the next tale.

Chapter 2

In the vibrant realm of internet gluttony, Jasmine reigned supreme as a YouTube mukbang sensation with a penchant for theatrics. Famous for her captivating videos and boundless energy, her channel was a haven for food enthusiasts seeking entertainment alongside their gastronomic adventures.

She sat in front of the camera, surrounded by a cornucopia of culinary delights and ready to devour three times the usual amount. Knowing the world was ending, she decided to do one last show before retreating to a bunker.

Eager to get started, she made her announcement and began with a colossal seafood spread, complete with generous servings of crab legs, shrimp, and lobster tails.

Dismissing some odd sounds coming from beyond her room as likely just noisy neighbors, she concealed her concerns and dug into the feast. She devoured most of it, but struggled to crack open some of the remaining shells. With mocking glances aimed at her audience through her video camera, she continued sucking down the food.

More strange noises from outside her room interrupted her mukbang madness. Jasmine, ever the dramatic diva, silenced the presumed audience with a finger to her lips, pretending to be in a suspenseful movie scene. However, her attempt at theatrics was cut short when she realized the racket was growing louder, and not in a good way. Her breath caught in her throat as she strained to listen over her chewing, her muscles tensing with unease. It sounded like... Running footsteps? But that was impossible, she lived alone.

With worry in her eyes, she stared into the camera, doing her best to ignore the commotion outside by overeating and putting on a show. With every glorious crack of a crayfish shell, she leaned closer to the lens, her excitement palpable as she showcased her culinary conquests. Each succulent bite of shrimp sent a tremor of pleasure down her back, her taste buds tingling with delight at the burst of briny sweetness.

But as hard as she tried, the background noise was getting to her. With a swift shake of her head, she dived in again and was transported to a world of gastronomic bliss, a sanctuary of flavors and textures where worries should have melted away. In spite of the distractions, she remained focused on her audience, using exaggerated gestures and animated expressions to turn her meal into a captivating spectacle for the eyes and ears of her viewers.

Her usual cadence and happy demeanor grew less apparent as she attempted to hide her concerns by shoving even more food into her mouth. Making a mess was something she wasn't used to. Juices dribbled down her chin as she wielded the crab legs like weapons, flinging bits of food in all directions. With a smirk directed at the lens, she sucked down the remaining meaty pieces, then moved on to the sticky honey-coated fried chicken.

With an occasional pause and a slight tilt of her head, she listened as the noises grew closer. Despite the escalating disturbance, she assured her audience not to worry and mentioned, between mouthfuls, her imminent retreat to a bunker. With another cheeky wink, she diverted her gaze from the camera and resumed eating. A quick swipe across her lips with one hand, and then with the other hand dove into the crispy skin.

She waved the wings around, and bits of meat and sauce flew everywhere. Some pieces landed on the table in front of her, while others ended up on her clothes and in her hair. She jumped when a sudden booming sound rattled her door, causing her heart to skip a beat with fear. For a moment, she hesitated, considering the possibility of danger lurking within her house.

Her eyes darting to the ring light, she quickly dismissed the idea, reassuring herself that she was safe in her room. However, a nagging realization crept into her consciousness—she hadn't prepared an escape plan in case things went south. Despite this unsettling awareness, she pushed it aside and resumed devouring the meal before her.

When groans sounded from beyond her bedroom and increased in volume, panic began to set in. To distract herself from the disconcerting noise, she moved to the noodles, consuming them with haste until her attention zeroed in on the camera with wide-eyed, fearful intensity.

Her messy hands, slick with sauce and crumbs, clawed at her throat as she fought for air, each gasp coming harder than the last. With a sense of desperation, she leaned forward, hoping the force of her movements would dislodge the obstructing food. But it remained willfully lodged, mocking her frantic efforts.

Her eyes widened in panic as the lack of oxygen became more pronounced. A strangled sound escaped her lips, and her face contorted into a shade of purple, blood vessels pulsing at her temples. In her distressed struggle, she inadvertently knocked her camera askew, tilting the image of her erratic actions.

With fear coursing through her veins, she took a deep breath, or at least attempted to, but it felt like sucking air through a straw clogged with thick syrup. Her vision blurred at the edges, darkness encroaching on her consciousness. Gathering every ounce of strength she had left, she hurled herself toward the door, her hand shaking as she gripped the doorknob and turned it.

When the door swung open, the zombies piled in. Mid-choke, the dead grasped at her. She twisted her body around, using a decaying corpse as a barrier, and attempted to mimic the Heimlich Maneuver. However, the undead had other plans. The creature gripped her torso and sank its teeth into her neck.

Along with the excruciating pain, the pressure of its hold on her dislodged the stuck food from her windpipe, allowing her to gasp for a much-needed lungful of air. With a heave, she managed to pull away from the zombie momentarily. But before she could escape, she was yanked back in.

In agony and bleeding, Jasmine surveyed her room one last time. Seafood, chicken, and noodles littered the walls, floor, and table—a chaotic aftermath of her mukbang session. With a tight grimace, she prepared herself for what would come next.

As the video concluded, Jasmine's appearance epitomized the delightful disarray of her room. Her clothes bore splashes of tartar sauce, and her hair was adorned with errant bits of shell. The tabletop, a demonstration of her indulgent dedication, was strewn with remnants of her feast.

With the lens capturing her final breath, Jasmine collapsed to the ground as the rotter released her. As she awaited her transformation, a thought surfaced. Would she still be able to film mukbangs in the afterlife? The idea of consuming human flesh on YouTube lingered in her mind as her eyes glazed over with a blinding, inky fog.

Zombie Movie & TV Trivia Answers: Round 1

1. A cemetery.
2. That was a trick question. No name was given. But fans labeled it 'Rage Virus' Within the movie it is simply referred to as 'virus or infection.'
3. Brad Pitt.
4. A cricket bat.
5. Cardio.
6. Monroeville Shopping Mall in Pennsylvania.
7. *Zombieland.*
8. Umbrella Corporation.
9. Yeon Sang-ho.
10. He has the ability to remember the memories of the humans he consumes.

Chapter 3

Peter's heart pounded against his chest like a drum as he raced through the unforgiving terrain of the rocky mountains, his boots kicking up clouds of dust with each frantic step. The harsh sunlight beat down upon him with unrelenting intensity, its scorching rays casting long shadows across the rugged landscape.

The stony ground offered little in the way of cover, and Peter could feel the oppressive heat pressing in on him from all sides. Sweat dripped down his brow, stinging his eyes as he squinted against the glare of the sun.

Behind him, the relentless growls of the undead pursued him like a pack of hungry wolves, their eerie cries echoing off the towering cliffs that loomed overhead. He knew he had to find a place to hide, a sanctuary where he could catch his breath and regroup before it was too late.

With desperation driving him forward, his eyes scanned the horizon for any sign of refuge. And that's when he spotted it—the entrance of an old coal mine nestled within the craggy peaks of the mountains, its yawning mouth beckoning to him like a beacon of hope.

Without hesitation, he veered off course and dashed toward the dark opening, his muscles burning with exertion as he pushed himself to his limits. The rocky terrain was treacherous beneath his feet, and more than once he stumbled and fell, losing his glasses and scraping his hands raw against the unforgiving surface of the rocks.

Devoid of his spectacles, his sight was reduced to almost nothing. Yet he pushed forward. He slipped into the cave and was immediately enveloped by darkness so thick, it was like plunging into fog. Panic surged through him like a bolt of lightning as he fumbled for his lighter, his trembling fingers struggling to find purchase on the small metal device.

With a flick of his wrist, the zippo ignited, casting a feeble glow that barely penetrated the inky blackness surrounding him. He held the flame aloft, its flickering light projecting eerie shadows on the walls of the cavern as he took hesitant steps forward, his heart hammering in his chest.

The air was thick with dust and the musty scent of decay, and Peter's stomach churned with a nauseating mixture of fear and revulsion. He pressed on, his footsteps echoing in the silence as he ventured deeper into the bowels of the earth.

After what felt like an eternity of stumbling through the darkness, his foot collided with something solid, sending him sprawling to the ground with a grunt of pain. Swearing under his breath, he picked himself up and dusted off his clothes. His fingers brushed against a wooden crate that had been hidden in the shadows.

Without hesitation, he pried open the lid and peered inside, his heart racing with anticipation. To his surprise, the box was filled with all manner of odds and ends, their surfaces coated with a thick layer of dust and grime.

But it was the item nestled at the bottom of the box that grabbed his attention. It was a dusty cylindrical object wrapped in brown paper, with a stubby bit of string protruding from one end. His brow furrowed in confusion as he picked it up, turning it over in his hands as he tried to make sense of what it could be.

The words printed on its side had long since faded, leaving behind nothing but a smudged blur of ink. Peter screwed up his face in concentration, racking his brain for any clue that could help him identify the mysterious item. With his poor eyesight, he thought it might be a candle, but the texture didn't feel like that of any wax candle he'd touched before.

Then, in a sudden flash of inspiration, it hit him—a cigar! That must be what it was, he thought to himself with a grin. Without hesitation, he used his lighter. He held it to the end of the object, waiting for it to catch fire and wondering if he should put the other end in his mouth and draw on it. As the flame licked at the paper, a sizzling sound reached Peter's ears. With his arm stretched out in front of him, he believed the noise he heard was due to its age of it, assuming the tobacco stick to be ancient.

Within seconds, pain shot through his hand as the fuse ignited the detonation. A deafening explosion echoed through the cave like thunder. Before he had a chance to react, the force of the blast sent him flying backward, his world spinning as he tumbled head over heels into the darkness.

While he lay there, dazed and disoriented and in agony, the acrid scent of smoke filled his nostrils. Peter realized with a sinking feeling in the pit of his stomach that he had made a grave mistake. With his hand blown off and a hole in his chest, he now understood that it wasn't what he first thought. Instead, it was a stick of TNT left behind by miners long gone.

With his last ounce of strength, he tried to push himself to his feet, but it was no use. His vision swam before his eyes, and darkness crept in at the edges of his consciousness as he succumbed to the inky blackness of the cave and whatever would come after.

Zombie Movie & TV Trivia: Round 2

1. What is the primary mode of transportation used by the survivors in *The Walking Dead*?
2. In what exotic setting does the zombie outbreak begin in *Dead Alive*?
3. What is the setting of the majority of the film *Pontypool*?
4. *Warm Bodies* is based on what novel, and by whom?
5. What is the primary objective of the player character in *Dead Rising*?
6. What iconic line is repeated throughout *Return of the Living Dead* regarding the zombies' desire to eat brains?
7. In *The Girl with All the Gifts,* what sets Melanie apart from other zombie-like creatures?
8. Who portrays the character Madeleine Short in the movie *White Zombie*?
9. Who played the role of Tallahassee in *Zombieland*?
10. What is the signature weapon used by Michonne in *The Walking Dead*?

Answers will be found after the next tale.

Chapter 4

In the midst of a zombie-infested world, Charlie frantically sifted through the scattered bags of provisions at the campsite. Everything he ever knew had devolved into mayhem, overrun by the ravenous undead. With each rustling movement, he couldn't shake the feeling of being watched by unseen eyes.

His hands moved with practiced speed, snatching up cans and packets of food as if his life depended on it—because it did. As he stuffed the last can into his knapsack, the tranquility of the forest shattered into chaos.

Bullets whizzed past his head, slicing through the air with deadly imprecision. But one of them found its mark. With instincts honed by survival, Charlie ducked and weaved through the overgrown grass, his breathing ragged as he sought cover. The clamor of gunfire deafened his senses, each shot like Russian roulette to him, a game of life and death.

In the pandemonium that ensued, the sounds of shooting acted as a siren call to the zombies lurking in the shadows. Drawn by the commotion, the deadheads wandered out of hiding, their groans mingling with the gunshots in a tornado of frightening noise.

While the gunmen were distracted by the onslaught of undead, Charlie seized the opportunity to make his escape. Through a haze of pain and the blur of his surroundings, his strength of will remained steady. Emerging from the dense foliage of the woods, he stumbled onto the desolate streets, his senses heightened by the threat of imminent danger. The abandoned area loomed before him, a manifestation of the destruction that had consumed the world.

Crashed cars littered the roadside, their twisted metal frames serving as evidence of death. Houses stood out like specters in the fading light, their windows and doors boarded up to guard them against the infected. He wondered for a brief moment if anyone was still living behind the barricaded homes he walked past. He doubted it, given how dilapidated they had become. The pavements were strewn with the remains of the fallen, their lifeless forms attracting flies, rodents, and birds.

Charlie limped through the deserted streets, his pulse racing in time with the throbbing of his injury. With each step, he drew closer to his destination, his mind fixated on the image of the rundown hospital he had passed hours earlier. The memory motivated him, propelling him forward despite the overwhelming odds he faced.

He stopped to tie his shirt around his gunshot wound and grimaced at the pain, then continued on as his vision began to blur further. Bugs filled the air, attracted to the lifeless bodies scattered on the pavement and their noxious smell. He glanced toward a house on the corner, where a lone zombie lurched and groaned in the front yard, much of its lower half missing as it clawed at the air.

Further down the road, another scene of horror awaited him. A rotter trapped inside a rusted car, its mangled hands clawing at the windows in a desperate bid for freedom. The sound of its rough moans reached Charlie's ears, making him nauseous, but he held down the bile. His gaze remained fixed dead ahead, his focus set on reaching the hospital.

With each step, his heart beat faster. The terror coursing through his veins was driving him forward despite the agony that wracked his body. He gritted his teeth against the pain, his willpower propelling his every move as he pressed on to the medical center.

As he approached the looming building, he couldn't help but be consumed by a sense of dread that washed over him. The formerly majestic front now existed as a deteriorating remnant of history, with shattered windows and decayed bricks and wood.

Weeks of overgrowth were reclaiming the structure, dissolving it into decay. With a shaky breath, he pushed open the doors and stepped inside, steeling himself for the horrors that awaited within.

Charlie's heart pounded like a drumbeat in his chest as he stumbled through the dark corridors of the abandoned hospital. Blood seeped from his bullet wound, leaving a crimson trail in his wake. The endless growls of the undead echoed in the distance, drawing closer with each passing moment. He was burdened with regret at his attempt to steal from other survivors He hadn't anticipated that they would shoot at him. If he hadn't been quick enough, another gunshot might have found its true mark—his head.

Desperation gnawed at his mind as he searched for a place to hide and tend to his injury. With every step, the pain in his leg intensified, sending waves of agony coursing through his body. He knew he couldn't outrun the zombies in his current state. He needed medical attention, and fast.

His breaths came in ragged gasps as he pushed open the door to one of the hospital's operating rooms, his eyes scanning all over for any sign of salvation. To his relief, he spotted an oddly yellow-colored scalpel lying on a nearby table, its edge glinting in the dim light. On a tray were bandages and half a bottle of hydrogen peroxide. In that moment, he believed he had hit the jackpot.

He staggered over to the table without hesitation, snatching up the blade. Though doubt briefly nagged at his mind, he forcibly suppressed it and plunged forward with resolve. He knew he had to act fast if he wanted any chance of survival.

With shaky hands, he sat on the operating table and began to slice through the fabric of his torn pants, revealing the extensive hole in his leg. Blood trickled from the wound, painting the floor with drops of a macabre shade of red. Ignoring the searing pain, he gritted his teeth and pressed the surgical knife against his flesh, bracing himself for what was to come next.

Inexperienced and lacking proper equipment, he knew he was taking a gamble by attempting to perform surgery. But with zombies closing in on his location, he had no other choice. Inhaling a deep breath, he made the first incision, his hands steady despite the fear coursing through his veins.

The scalpel sliced through his skin like a laser through a sheet of paper, eliciting a guttural cry of pain from Charlie's lips. Blood pooled around him, staining his clothes and dripping onto the operating table. But Charlie pressed on, consumed by a singular focus, survival.

With each slice of the instrument, his stomach began to knot, and his movements grew sluggish. The throbbing in his leg threatened to overwhelm him, but he fought through it with grim determination born of desperation. Probing with a finger, he rummaged about in search of the bullet. Unable to find it, he knew he had to cut deeper.

But then, disaster struck. In his haste and panic, he accidentally severed an artery, unleashing a torrent of blood that he was powerless to stop. Alarm surged through him like a tidal wave as he realized the gravity of his mistake. His vision darkened, and blackness crept in at the edges of his consciousness.

The sound of approaching disjointed footsteps jolted him back to reality. With a sinking feeling in the pit of his stomach, he became aware that the zombies were almost upon him. He had failed in his desperate bid for survival, and now he would pay the ultimate price.

Zombie Movie & TV Trivia Answers: Round 2

1. On foot.
2. The zombie outbreak begins in the Rat-Monkey Exhibit at the Wellington Zoo.
3. *Pontypool* takes place in a radio station located in the small town of Pontypool, Ontario, Canada.
4. Isaac Marion.
5. The primary objective of the player character is to survive the zombie outbreak while completing various missions and rescuing survivors.
6. "Brains! More brains!"
7. She retains her ability to think and learn.
8. Madge Bellamy.
9. Woody Harrelson.
10. A katana.

Chapter 5

Geoffrey's wild scramble through the meadow unfurled like a daisy-strewn tapestry. Each petal was a feathery wisp of hopelessness as he deftly maneuvered through the incessant zombie horde. Panic and determination melded, weaving together like the intricate, interlocking pieces of a jigsaw puzzle.

His frantic heartbeat pounded against his ribs, synchronized with a pulsing rhythm emanating from his neck that created a powerful surge of adrenaline that fueled his every move. It was as though uncertainty and resolve had assembled as one, completing the mosaic of his emotions.

Hurrying through the chaotic grassland toward a forest, he sought refuge from the hungry abominations with their odd, mismatched movements. Rushing through the landscape, his vision landed on a few trees ahead, and something large dangling from a branch. Drawn to it like a spider to a fly, he sprinted harder. When he was near the trunk, he was able to discern what it was, and it gave him an idea. He stopped running, looked back to catch sight of where the freshly turned zombies were, and was satisfied he had time.

He climbed a tree and got above the hive he had spotted. When the zombies got close enough, he would drop it on their heads, a plan he believed was foolproof. The rotters chasing him were unable to find him and started to walk in circles. So he called out to them, "Hey dumbasses, I'm up here!" and threw some twigs down. But they were too light and fell silently.

"Come on, shitheads, I'm right here!" he yelled repeatedly. Each time, the living dead would snap their decaying mouths at the source of the noise. But unable to figure out where it was coming from, they would continue moving about, getting farther away from where Geoff needed them to be.

Without their apparent inability to look up, he had to come up with another plan. He eyed the hive, and a lightbulb moment struck him. He lowered his body enough to reach the hive and wriggled it free from the branch.

He carefully he descended from the tree with the hive. As soon as his feet touched the grass, he called out to some creatures that were ambling away. "Here! I'm over here! Come and get me!" he said. He watched as they made their way toward him, giving him the chance to ready his aim. He took a single step back, spread his legs a little, and raised his arm, ready to throw the hive.

A few of the bees didn't like the sudden movements and flew out, landing on his outstretched hand and stinging him. In his panic, he rushed forward and his foot collided with a boulder. He inadvertently launched the hive into the air, and it came crashing down upon his own head, enveloping him in a swirling storm of angry pollinators. The buzzing horde, once sufficiently disturbed, retaliated with a vengeance.

Running around now in frenzied circles, he resembled a tumultuous whirlwind, the hive serving as both a helmet and a tormentor. A million tiny assailants unleashed their fury, stingers finding their mark on every inch of his face. The humming reached a deafening crescendo, punctuated by his yelps and the furious buzz of the swarm.

With his vision obscured, he swatted and flailed with rage, trying to free his head from the clinging mass of bees. The incessant murmur and stinging only added to his misery.

Fumbling blindly, he collided with a hungry zombie. The impact shattered the hive into fragments, further enraging the already irate insects. The liberated colony swirled around in disarray, a frenzied cloud of angry black-and-yellow flyers seeking revenge for their disrupted abode. Seizing an opportunity, the buzzers swooped into the open mouth of the undead.

Freed but disoriented, Geoff's body gave way, and he took a dramatic fall. Lying on the ground with puffy eyes, he could only stare in disbelief. The reanimated ones, with mouths full of stingers, began to swell like balloons. Geoff was flabbergasted. How could their dead bodies react? It was a conundrum to him. He continued to view them as best he could in his nearly blind state. They banged into one another, and one transformed into a roly-poly mass, careening down the hill.

A bizarre sight unfolded like a ludicrous game of bowling, with the swollen abomination knocking its ghoul brethren around like ten-pins. The biters tumbled and flailed as the swollen-mouthed roamers continued their inadvertent rampage, propelled by the bees within. The collision of the risen created a grim background of moans, groans, and the persistent hum of enraged honeybees.

In Geoffery's last moments, amidst the agonizing and absurd theatrics, he felt a single bee crawl out from beneath his eyelid. As if to mock him, it stung him before flapping its wings, only to discover it couldn't, and died on his face. In that moment, he attempted to cry and scream, but his own swollen mouth rendered him incapable.

His throat began to close, suffocating him as if a vise was tightening around his neck. Venom flowed through his veins, and the swelling from the thousands of bites caused his body to expand as well, resembling the Goodyear blimp. He closed his eyes with the sound of angry humming still ringing in his ears.

Zombie Movie & TV Trivia: Round 3

1. What is the main character's name in the classic film *Night of the Living Dead*?
2. What popular British breakfast item does Shaun use to kill a zombie in his back yard?
3. What activity do "R" and Julie engage in together that helps "R" regain his humanity in *Warm Bodies*?
4. Who directed the 1979 film *Zombi 2,* which is known for its graphic and shocking scenes?
5. What is the name of the infected zones in the film *Monsters,* where extraterrestrial life forms turn people into zombie-like creatures?
6. In *Train to Busan,* what kind of transportation do the survivors use to escape the zombie apocalypse?
7. What year was *Night of the Living Dead* released?
8. What is the title of the 2004 horror-comedy film starring Simon Pegg and Nick Frost, which involves a rural village battling zombies?
9. In *World War Z,* where does Gerry Lane (Brad Pitt) travel to find a potential cure for the zombie pandemic?
10. Which 1981 film, directed by Sam Raimi, combines horror with comedy and features a group of friends vacationing in a cabin?

Answers will be found after the next tale.

Chapter 6

Embark on an extraordinary odyssey through the life of Joe. He was a five-hundred-pound twenty-two-year-old whose existence was an intricate pattern woven within the cocoon of his bed. Born with a thyroid disease that had consigned him to a life of limited mobility, his journey unfolded against a backdrop of streaming services, snack-strewn landscapes, and the melodic hum of his beloved video games.

His devoted mother, a paragon of caregiving, catered to his every need, and this day was no different. She busied herself in the kitchen making his favorite dinner, mac-n-cheese.

As the evening sun cast a warm glow through Joe's perpetually drawn curtains, his mom endeavored to craft the perfect cheesy delight—a culinary masterpiece intended to satisfy the epicurean cravings of her bedridden son. The aromas wafted through the air, creating an illusion of normalcy in a world that was teetering on the brink of the extraordinary.

However, fate had other plans for Joe, whose universe of digital escapes was about to intersect with the grim reality unfolding in the neighborhood. Outside, the once recognizable voices of locals had transformed into a cacophony of desperation and terror. Unperturbed, he remained cocooned in his haven, his domain still echoing with the familiar click-clack of controller buttons and the muffled hubbub of his mom's bustling activities.

His mom delivered his perfect macaroni and cheese, leaving the plate on his side table. To get his attention, she tapped him on the shoulder. He paused his play long enough to waggle a stubby finger in gratitude. She smiled and left.

In the hallway, she detected the sounds of screaming. At first, she thought it was one of the games her son was playing. Then it became too close, too real, and so she headed for the back door to investigate.

The door creaked open and his mother stepped outdoors to inspect the source of the screams. Beyond their humble house, the neighborhood had become a stage of ghoulish frenzy, with neighbors succumbing to the insidious bites of the zombie contagion. But the noises didn't reach Joe's room. He remained immersed in a virtual realm of beating up otherworldly monsters, ignorant of the impending storm.

His beloved mom was bitten and transformed into an undead entity. She lurched back into the house with an insatiable hunger for the warmth of the living. She banged into furniture, heading for the source of some vibrations, her decaying hands groping in search of the elusive prey.

She caught the muffled thuds and excited voice of someone within the house. With intermittent bursts of sound emanating from Joe's flickering screen, a green glow flashed underneath the gap of the door. She narrowed in, drawn to the unknown sounds.

Joe, frustrated by a sudden power outage, yelled, "Mom, did you forget to pay the electricity bill again? Mom, answer me!"

Mesmerized by the human's vocalizations, she leaned on the door and it swung open. She was drooling for his flesh. She fumbled for his body, covered in layers of blankets. He barely recognized her.

"Mom is that you?" She didn't answer. "Mom, what the hell!" He reached over and grabbed the plate of macaroni. He blinked at the corpse-woman trying to grab at him. Then he understood what is happening, but wouldn't accept it. "Mom, enough with the tricks. Get out of my room!"

When she didn't leave and instead opened her mouth, he realized that this is very real and that his mother has turned into one of the living dead. He eyed his baseball bat in the corner of his room.

She pulled at the bedding and tugged at the covers, her decaying hands groping for his skin. Every time she made a grab at him, she fell to the floor, unable to retain purchase. Surprised by the hunger she had for him, he stared blankly at her. The clash between his gargantuan physique and the newfound undead vigor of his old mother took on a gruesome dichotomy.

"There's a baseball bat over there... Why the hell don't I drop this plate and take hold of the bat? But I'm hungry... Nah, c'mon, drop the mac-n-cheese. But it's my favorite... Why is my body not responding to what I want it to do? DROP FOOD, GRAB BASEBALL BAT! She's almost got me! Why am I still holding this... ARRRGHGHAGHAGHH!"

As he valiantly tried to fend off the zombified advances of his once-loving mom, he began to pant and gasp for breath. The sudden movements and erratic strenuous efforts rendered him exhausted, and he couldn't fight her off. She sank her teeth into the side of his face, turning him into the meal of a lifetime.

Zombie Movie & TV Trivia Answers: Round 3

1. Ben.
2. Shaun uses a vinyl record of the album "OK Computer" by Radiohead to decapitate a zombie in his back yard.
3. "R" and Julie engage in various activities such as listening to music, playing vinyl records, and spending time together, which helps "R" regain his humanity.
4. Lucio Fulci.
5. Infected Zones.
6. A train.
7. *Night of the Living Dead* was released in 1968.
8. *Shaun of the Dead.*
9. Israel.
10. *The Evil Dead.*

Chapter 7

Catarina, a spirited ninety-year-old resident of the retirement village, found herself in the midst of a surreal and terrifying situation as chaos erupted in the once peaceful corridors of the nursing home. The cacophony of screams and groans echoed off the sterile walls, mingling with the panicked shuffling of residents and the guttural growls of the zombies.

With her trusty walker by her side, Cat's first instinct was to flee. However, the zombie nurse, her former caregiver but now a ravenous undead creature, had other plans. With a throaty growl, it lurched towards her, its outstretched arms reaching for her frail form.

Her heart pounded as she surveyed her surroundings, searching for an escape route. With a quick glance over her shoulder, she spotted a nearby linen wardrobe and headed for it, her mobility aid clattering along the linoleum floor before her.

The deadhead, meanwhile, stumbled clumsily in pursuit, its decaying limbs unable to match her nimble movements. It crashed into walls, tripped over furnishings, and emitted frustrated groans as Cat continually evaded its grasp.

Unable to open the locked cupboard, she went down the hall. At each turn of the hallway, she executed daring maneuvers—weaving in and out of rooms, ducking around furniture, and even employing her walker as an improvised obstacle. She ducked under a wayward IV stand, narrowly avoiding the undead nurse's outstretched arms as it faltered past.

As they rounded a corner, she spotted an opportunity. With a swift movement, she maneuvered her walker in front of her, causing the ghoul to stumble and fall to the ground with a resounding crash.

But Cat's relief was short-lived as she realized her mistake. In her haste, she had backed herself into a dead-end corridor with no means of escape. The reanimated corpse, undeterred by its fall, quickly regained its footing and turned to face her, its milky eyes fixed on its prey.

With a sinking sensation in her stomach, Cat realized she had only moments to act. She frantically searched the walls for any sign of a hidden door, but the sterile passageway offered no sanctuary.

Desperation fueled her actions as she shifted her walker and faced the opposite wall. Hanging there was a bright red fire extinguisher, which gave her an idea. With trembling hands she latched onto it. Its cold, metallic form nestled in her grip, she removed it and inspected it. She struggled to pull the safety pin. The zombie nurse drew closer, its rasping breaths growing louder with each passing second.

Finally, with a triumphant yank, the peg popped free, and she braced herself for the inevitable confrontation. But as she pressed down on the handle, expecting a controlled burst of foam to incapacitate her assailant, she was met with an unexpected surge of pressure that sent her reeling backward.

Like a pendulum swinging wildly out of control, she careened across the corridor, the force of the suds propelling her with alarming speed. She swung back and forth in a dizzying arc, her walker clattering behind her as she struggled to maintain her balance.

The foam sprayed in all directions, coating the walls and floor in a slick, white sheen. The zombie nurse, caught off-guard by the sudden onslaught, staggered back, its outstretched arms flailing in a futile attempt to ward off the froth.

But Cat's wild ride came to an abrupt end as she collided with a nearby wall with bone-jarring force. The impact knocked the breath from her lungs, leaving her dazed and disoriented on the cold linoleum surface.

As the stuff settled and the chaos subsided, Cat lay motionless on the ground, her chest rising and falling in shallow gasps. As she drifted into unconsciousness, she couldn't help but wonder if there had been a better way—a simpler way—to meet her end.

A twinkle in her eye remained, though. With a wry smile and one final breath, she muttered her parting words. "Well, at least I beat you at bingo."

The once bustling retirement home was then silent, save for the distant moans of the undead echoing through the corridors.

Zombie Movie & TV Trivia: Round 4

1. What is the primary cause of the zombie outbreak in the Spanish horror film *[*REC]* (2007)?
2. In *Planet Terror,* part of the *Grindhouse* double feature, what unusual weapon does Cherry Darling (Rose McGowan) have?
3. Which 2019 film, directed by Jim Jarmusch, stars Bill Murray and Adam Driver as small-town police officers facing a zombie uprising?
4. In *28 Weeks Later,* what is the key to a potential immunity to the Rage virus?
5. What is the destination of the train in *Train to Busan*?
6. Which George A. Romero film is often considered the first feature-length zombie film and was released in 1968?
7. In the video game series *Resident Evil* (on which the movies were based), what is the name of the fictional city where the T-virus outbreak occurs?
8. What is the name of the island in *Dead Snow* where a group of friends encounters Nazi zombies?
9. Which 2009 film, directed by Ruben Fleischer, follows a group of survivors navigating a world overrun by zombies?
10. What is the nickname given to the intelligent zombie in *Land of the Dead* (2005)?

Answers will be found after the next tale.

Chapter 8

Bob, 28, was an unwavering nature enthusiast whose grasp on escape routes was as shaky as his balance. He spotted a group of tall trees nearby and made his way there. Standing under the canopy, he contemplated scaling one of them. Then he chickened out, until his mind was made up for him when a horde of the undead drew closer.

He began his ascent up the maple tree, his heart racing with a mix of fear and determination. The rough bark of the trunk scratched his palms as he reached for each next handhold, leaving behind a lingering scent of earthy wood. With each upward movement, his muscles strained against the weight of his body. The sound of his heavy breathing filled the air around him, mingling with the rustle of foliage and the distant moans of the approaching zombies.

The cool breeze carried the fragrance of pine needles and damp soil, heightening Bob's senses as he climbed higher. The leaves above him fluttered about, casting dappled shadows across his face. Sweat beaded on his forehead, trickling down his neck and blending with the dirt and grime accumulated from his frantic escape through the wilderness.

Despite his best efforts to maintain his balance, his movements were awkward and uncoordinated, resembling the clumsy antics of a drunken acrobat. Twigs snapped underfoot and loose debris scattered with each step, creating strident sounds that echoed through the silent forest.

All of a sudden, Bob froze as he sensed a disturbance nearby. His ears picked up the faint noise of scales sliding against bark, followed by a low hiss that made his hair stand on end. He glanced to his left and spotted the source of the sound—a disgruntled snake, its skin shimmering in the dappled sunlight as it coiled and uncoiled in agitation.

Bob's heart skipped a beat as he realized that by accident he'd trespassed into the snake's territory. He inched away, hoping to avoid provoking the creature further, but his movements only seemed to agitate it more. The serpent's eyes fixated on him with an intensity that sent a chill down his back, and he knew he must tread with extreme caution to avoid being bitten.

Mid-climb, Bob froze in sheer terror as he locked eyes with the disturbed snake. His breath caught in his throat, and he held it as if the slightest exhale might provoke the animal. The air around him felt charged with tension, and he could hear the thud of his heart pounding in his ears, drowning out all other sounds.

The reptile, surprised by Bob's sudden stillness, did its best to live up to its reputation. With a flick of its tongue, it assessed the situation before deciding on its next move. In a series of sinuous movements, it maneuvered itself away from the branch it had earlier occupied, its scales glinting in the speckled sunlight filtering through the canopy above.

While it slithered along the branches, Bob remained motionless, his muscles tensed with anticipation. He could detect the rough texture of the bark pressing against his palms and the abrasive edges of the leaves brushing over his skin. The scent of damp earth and pine needles filled his nostrils, mingling with the faint odor of the snake's musk.

With bated breath, he gazed as the viper inched closer, its body undulating and graceful with each movement. He could sense the subtle vibration of its scales along the wood as it passed over him, sending a shiver through him. The sensation was both eerie and exhilarating, heightening his senses to the world around him.

As it reached the other side of the branch and continued its descent down the tree, he released the breath he had been holding and let out a sigh of relief. The tension in the air dissipated, replaced by a feeling of cautious calm. He watched the serpent disappear into the foliage below, grateful for the brief reprieve from the dangers lurking in the forest.

For a moment, he believed he was somehow being spared by the whims of fate. A mocking grin crossed his face as he carried on with his ascent. He reached a sturdy branch and took a victorious inhale. But his victory was short-lived when he witnessed the sky darken. Ominous clouds gathered, and he wondered if the rain he anticipated would cause him to slip. Unfazed, he undid his belt, looping one end around his right wrist and the other over the bough, confident that it would secure him against potential slips.

Then a crack pierced the air as a bolt of lightning targeted the very tree he was precariously perched on. Now, in addition to the relentless pursuit by the zombies, Bob found himself sitting atop a rapidly burning branch.

In frantic moves, he tried to untether his arm. Flames licked dangerously close to his hand as he unhooked the buckle. Panic set in as he realized that the dual threats of fiery doom and the hungry undead were closing in on him faster than he'd anticipated.

In a desperate attempt to escape his sizzling perch, he executed a less-than-graceful dive to the ground. Limbs swung in all directions as he tumbled down. The zombies swooped in and hungrily feasted on him. The tree, now ablaze, stood as a charred witness to his ill-fated survival strategy.

Zombie Movie & TV Trivia Answers: Round 4

1. A demonic possession.
2. A machine-gun leg.
3. *The Dead Don't Die.*
4. Natural immunity.
5. The destination of the train is the city of Busan in South Korea.
6. *Night of the Living Dead.*
7. Raccoon City.
8. Øksfjord.
9. *Zombieland.*
10. Big Daddy.

Chapter 9

In the heart of the zombie apocalypse, let's meet Sarah, an audacious soul who happens to have a unique perspective—she's not nearsighted, farsighted, or any kind of "sighted" at all. No, she's a proud card-carrying member of the 100 Percent Blind Club.

Sarah's day began like any other, with the sun casting its warm glow over the once-familiar neighborhood. Inside her modest house, the usual sounds of the morning filled the air—the hum of appliances, the creak of floorboards, and the faint chirping of birds outdoors.

As she went about her routine, her heightened sense of hearing picked up subtle changes in the atmosphere—a distant shuffle here, a muffled groan there. However, Sarah, ever the optimist, dismissed these noises as nothing more than the typical background noise of urban life.

It wasn't until she stepped outside her front door that the reality of her circumstances hit her like a ton of bricks. The once-familiar streets were now overrun with hordes of the undead, their eerie moans echoing through the city. Panic seized her as she deduced the gravity of the situation. With her heart racing and her mind whirling even faster, she realized she had to act fast if she wanted to survive.

Equipped with determination and a heightened sense of hearing, Sarah's adrenaline kicked into overdrive as she listened to the chaos unfolding around her. The ground beneath her feet felt solid and familiar, but the air was thick with the stench of decay and desperation. With each passing moment, the tension in the atmosphere grew palpable, like a tornado brewing on the horizon.

As she stood on the threshold of her once-cozy home, her mind raced with possibilities. Should she stay and barricade herself inside, hoping to ride out the storm? Or should she take her chances out in the open, braving the dangers of the outside world in search of help?

In the end, her adventurous spirit won out over her better judgment. With a deep breath and a firm resolve, she made the critical decision to venture out into the unknown, armed only with her wits and her unwavering determination to survive.

Her super-sensitive ears became the lead conductors in a wild melody of undead moans and shuffling footsteps. The ground beneath her feet was like a musical score, guiding her through the lawns of unsuspecting neighbors. Dodging obstacles? Easy-peasy—she was practically a ninja of the echo universe.

As she maneuvered through the labyrinth of grass, the crazed wails reached a crescendo and her finely-tuned hearing sensed the approaching horde. The chaotic biters' uproar peaked, creating a dissonant harmony that only Sarah could interpret. With her ears as her eyes, she sprinted with unbridled confidence, her nervous and now slightly unhinged laughter echoing through the eerie soundscape.

Fully aware of the encroaching army of the dead, her perceptions transformed the slurred groaning into a zombified mariachi band that emerged from the shadows, adding an unintentional soundtrack to her escapade. The zombie musicians, missing a few limbs but determined to serenade the apocalypse, followed her like a bizarre fan club.

Thinking she was safe from cars—heck, she hadn't detected any motors roaring—she decided to take her erratic moves to the streets. As she twirled through the intersection, blindly unaware of the oncoming traffic, the once-muted growl of engines grew, vibrating through the surroundings and into her bones. The rumble of tires on pavement became a deafening roar, each car adding its unique clamor to the chorus of chaos.

Barefoot, she stood like the fearless maestro of her own disaster, enduring the rough texture of the road beneath her feet as she swayed to the rhythm of the approaching vehicles. The acrid scent of burning rubber filled her nostrils, mixing with the metallic tang of gasoline fumes that hung heavy in the air. A woosh of wind rushed past her when a van passed by. She tried to get her bearings, but turned the wrong way.

All of a sudden, another car joined the ensemble with a deafening roar, its headlights bearing down on her like the spotlight of an unwelcome stage. The collision was like the grand finale of a circus act, the screech of brakes and the crunch of metal blending with her own panicked gasps. She tumbled to the pavement, the impact jolting through her body as she crashed to the ground.

Her anxious chuckling, now even more untamed, echoed through the silent city, mingling with the distant wail of sirens. The scent of blood and burning rubber filled her senses as she lay motionless on the asphalt, the final note in the climax of her chaos.

Zombie Movie & TV Trivia: Round 5

1. In *Dawn of the Dead* (1978), what does the group of survivors use as a form of transportation to reach the shopping mall?
2. How do the infected individuals behave in *The Crazies* (2010)?
3. Who directed the 2018 South Korean film *Rampant,* which combines historical drama with a zombie apocalypse?
4. Who created the TV series *Dead Set*?
5. What is the name of the protagonist, a young girl with a unique condition, in *The Girl with All the Gifts*?
6. In *I Am Legend,* what is the protagonist's name and occupation before the apocalypse?
7. Who directed the movie *Re-Animator*?
8. What is the title of the 2016 South Korean animated film that tells the story of a zombie apocalypse from the perspective of a zombie?
9. In *World War Z,* what distinctive sound is associated with the infected individuals and serves as an early warning sign of their presence?
10. What is the primary location for the events in the film *Pontypool* (2008)?

Answers will be found after the next tale.

Chapter 10

Max, a man of daring exploits with a heart as golden as a sunflower, found himself in the chaotic clutches of the zombie apocalypse armed with an escape plan as unconventional as his spirit—the trusty companion of his adventures, a roaring motorcycle. The rotters lurked close by, making their way toward him, their intentions obscured by his lack of auditory awareness.

He sat on his motorbike with determination gleaming in his eyes. He sensed the vibrations resonate through his hands as he revved up the engine. The acrid smell of gasoline permeated the air, mingling with the faint scent of decay wafting from the neighboring undead. Nostrils flaring, he inhaled deeply, steeling himself for the perilous journey ahead.

Checking the fuel gauge and finding it low, he switched off the motor, grabbed a can, and embarked on foot to a nearby gas station. Walking with extreme caution through the eerily quiet streets, he reached the dilapidated station and located a rusted pump. He filled up his container with urgency, his gaze lingering on the surrounding area.

As he screwed the cap back on the can, his eyes darted around for any signs of movement. A sudden motion caught his eye. Turning, he spotted an animated corpse lurching toward him, its decaying flesh barely holding together. Reacting on instinct, he grabbed the gas nozzle and aimed it at the approaching zombie, dousing it with gasoline. Retrieving a lighter from his pocket, he ignited it with a flick of his thumb and hurled the flame at the rotter, setting fire to it and the pumps. The explosion echoed through the deserted area as Max made a hasty retreat back.

Though fully aware of the world collapsing around him and disrupting his otherwise normal life, he had dreams to pursue. While he prepared his escape and readied his bike, his keen eyes witnessed an approaching shambler that hurried him along. He felt a bead of sweat trickle down his forehead, the warmth contrasting with the chill of anticipation coursing through his veins.

Without a moment's hesitation, he straddled his trusty motorbike and accelerated down the desolate streets, confident that his motorized steed would grant him a swift getaway. The rush of wind against his skin, carrying with it the faint scent of distant smoke and the tang of metal, powered his adrenaline-fueled flight. Pausing for a second to contemplate his route, his head turned away from the broken mirrors on his cycle. Born deaf and thus relying on his other senses, he failed to detect the zombie clambering onto the back wheel.

Cruising at what he believed to be an acceptable pace to outwit the pursuing flesh-eaters, he navigated the thoroughfares, unaware of the ghoul stowaway clinging to the back of his Harley like an undead hitchhiker on an unconventional journey.

The abomination gripped the motorcycle with a tenacity propelled by hunger, showcasing a peculiar skill despite its grotesque form. Its limbs flailed in a deformed spin cycle reminiscent of a malfunctioning washing machine. Max was unable to hear the noises emanating from the rotting traveler, which were loud enough to wake the dormant dead.

Ahead of him a group of the infected had occupied the road. In a daring display of agility, he executed a series of evasive maneuvers. He darted and weaved between the lumbering zombies like a daredevil on wheels, narrowly avoiding their grasping hands with each calculated twist and turn. He was confident in his ability to outsmart the infected. But his reanimated passenger, with extremities swinging like a demented helicopter, was gaining ground on him.

With one disfigured arm gripping the frame and the other engaged in a bizarre grabbing act of doom, the deadhead reached, snatched, and latched onto Max, yanking him backward with unexpected force. The motorcycle spun out of control, toppling over and pinning him underneath, while the ghoul, thrown off in the accident, managed a slow, uncoordinated uprising.

Not wanting to be bitten, Max shoved the bike off his body and scrambled out of the way, his heart pounding with urgency. Limping along the desolate roads, he sought refuge and came across a fenced field. Before he climbed over the fence, he gazed at a weathered sign that read, 'Warning! Uncleared Minefield!' Despite the clear caution, he scoffed and dismissed it as a desperate attempt to deter surviving travelers.

With a reckless disregard for his safety, he hobbled over the barrier and pushed onward, eager to put distance between himself and the pursuing zombie. Halfway through the pasture, he felt a sudden shift beneath his boot, along with a subtle but unmistakable pressure against the sole of his shoe. In a moment of horrifying realization, he lifted his foot to run, which triggered a hidden mine that propelled him sky-high, sealing his fate in an explosive climax within his silent world.

Zombie Movie & TV Trivia Answers: Round 5

1. A helicopter.
2. The infected individuals exhibit violent and unpredictable behavior.
3. Kim Sung-hoon.
4. *Dead Set* was created by Charlie Brooker.
5. The name of the protagonist is Melanie.
6. Robert Neville, a virologist.
7. Stuart Gordon.
8. Seoul Station.
9. They emit a distinct clicking noise similar to that of insects, which becomes an eerie harbinger of their impending attack.
10. A radio station.

Chapter 11

Lily, a woman with an insatiable sweet tooth and diabetes, found herself in a predicament amid a zombie apocalypse. Amidst the chaos, beads of sweat formed on her forehead as she weighed her options. Realizing that her primary goal should be securing insulin, she set her sights on the nearest pharmacy. Ignoring the imminent danger, she darted through the desolate roads, her urgency propelled not just by a need for survival but by the desperate quest for life-saving medication.

As Lily hurried through the deserted streets, the world around her seemed to blur into a frenzy of muted colors and indistinct shapes. The cacophony of her pounding heart drowned out the eerie silence of the apocalypse. Sweat trickled down her face, leaving a salty trail that stung her eyes. Her breaths came in ragged gasps, the air thick with a metallic tang that clung to her throat.

With each step, Lily's senses were assaulted by the powerful onslaught of her impending diabetic crisis. Her perspiration-soaked clothes emitted a sickly sweet scent that, when mixed with the stench of decay, created an overwhelming and nauseating cocktail. Her mouth turned dry and gluey, a barren desert lacking moisture.

As she stumbled towards the pharmacy, her vision began to swim, the world tilting and spinning around her in a dizzying whirlwind. Taunting and elusive, shadows moved at the edges of her eyesight. The sound of her own voice become a distant whisper, lost in the confusion of her thoughts.

Panic clawed at her as a primal instinct urged her to flee, to find safety before it was too late. But she knew that she couldn't afford to give in to fear, not when her life hung in the balance. With trembling hands, she reached for her last remaining vial of insulin, a lifeline in the heart of the storm.

As she injected the medication into her thigh, a wave of relief washed over her, the cool rush of the liquid soothing her frayed nerves. Over time the world around her began to come back into focus. The colors regained their vibrancy, the shapes solidifying into tangible forms.

With newfound strength coursing through her veins, she rose to her feet, her eyes burning with unwavering resolve. Understanding that she couldn't stay hidden forever, she recognized the need to locate more insulin in order to survive. And so she continued on, in search of additional life-saving medication.

Dismayed by the barren counters of the drugstore she came across, Lily sprinted through the abandoned streets in pursuit of another store. The sight that awaited her at the second one was just as disheartening—shelves ransacked, an aftermath of the undead rampage. Panic set in, and she had to think on her feet. She spent hours searching, only to come up empty.

A day went by, and she had no luck in finding any more insulin. The realization dawned on her that none would be found, as every medication of all kinds had already been pillaged. Considering her circumstances, she was compelled to shift her focus to her Plan B, stockpiling sweets.

Dashing into a local shop, she collected an armful of candy, chocolates, and sugary delights. Convincing herself that she was safe behind the sturdy walls, armed with her bunch of treats, she taunted the zombies. Sticking her tongue out, she winked at the infected ambulating towards her. Their lethargic pace gave her the precious time she needed. Leaving the store, she made her way to another structure.

Before heading inside, she made faces at the lingering deadheads, giving them a cheeky wink, and then she entered the premises, dumping her stash like a resourceful squirrel. With her recently acquired treasure trove, she locked herself in. She glanced through the barricaded windows, her eyes meeting the slow, relentless approach of the zombie horde she had attracted.

Convinced of her security, she took a nap, unaware that the building was not as sturdy as she had thought. As Lily's eyelids fluttered in a restless slumber, the silence of the deserted building was shattered by a sudden crash. Her eyes flew wide, her heart racing as a surge of apprehension gripped her. The door groaned under the force of the impact, threatening to give way.

With a surge of alarm, she scrambled to her feet, her mind racing as she surveyed the place for an escape route. But before she was able to take action, the door exploded inward, splinters flying in all directions as the infected burst into the room. Time seemed to slow to a crawl as her survival instincts kicked into overdrive. Without hesitation, she reached for the nearest weapon at hand—a handful of candies she had collected earlier. Gripping them, she flung them at the oncoming threat with all the force she could muster.

The confections struck the first deadhead with a sickening gloopy thud, lodging in its decayed flesh and causing it to recoil in surprise. Lily seized the opportunity, lashing out with whatever makeshift weapons she could find—a broken broom handle, a shattered piece of furniture—anything to keep the creature at bay. She ducked and weaved to avoid the grasping hands of the undead, which now resembled a life-size piñata.

With a surge of desperation, she grabbed a supersized chocolate log. Its aroma tantalized her taste buds, and in a moment of sweet temptation she couldn't resist taking a bite. As the rich savor flooded her senses, she experienced a rush of energy coursing through her veins, the sweetness providing a much-needed boost to her flagging strength.

While she licked her lips, lost in a momentary bliss of indulgence, the infected one surged forward, its decayed form crashing into her with unexpected force. Stuck together in a tangled mess of goo and decay, Lily and the undead struggled in a bizarre sticky embrace. The creature's rotten mouth latched onto her cheek, its decaying teeth sinking into her flesh with a sickening slurp.

Lying there, the realization of her demise sank in. Her only regret was not having more reliable weapons.

Zombie Movie & TV Trivia: Round 6

1. Who directed the 2004 remake of *Dawn of the Dead*?
2. What is the name of the protagonist and former sheriff's deputy who leads the group of survivors in *The Walking Dead*?
3. Who directed the 1993 comedy-horror film *My Boyfriend's Back*?
4. In *Maggie* (2015), what is the name of Arnold Schwarzenegger's character, who cares for his infected daughter?
5. What is the objective of the main characters in the film *The Battery* (2012) during the zombie apocalypse?
6. In the 1990 film *Night of the Living Dead,* what significant change did director Tom Savini make to Barbara's character?
7. What is the name of the virus in *[*REC]²* that turns people into aggressive, demonic creatures?
8. Who directed the 2014 Australian film *Wyrmwood: Road of the Dead*?
9. What is the term used to describe the fast-moving zombies in *World War Z*?
10. What is the name of the character who provides comedic relief in *Zombieland* and is obsessed with finding Twinkies?

Answers will be found after the next tale.

Chapter 12

Nineteen-year-old Wendy, fueled by dreams of running, found herself in the heart of a zombie apocalypse. Unable to outpace the army of the dead and disadvantaged by her asthma, which stressed her out, she also had only one inhaler left. With this limitation, she had no choice but to be extra careful.

With her nebulizer clutched in hand, she took off down the abandoned streets, ducking groping hands, sideswiping rotting bodies, and avoiding tripping over rubbish. Her lungs squeezed tightly around her ribs, a pressure building in her upper airways threatening to stop her breathing. She took a moment's pause, inhaled deeply from her puffer, and carried on.

As Wendy sprinted through the desolate roads, her senses were on high alert, attuned to every sight, sound, and scent of the decaying world surrounding her. The putrid stench of dead flesh hung heavy in the air, assaulting her nostrils with its nauseating aroma. Each step she took echoed through the empty lanes, her racing heartbeat a constant drumbeat of fear in her ears.

Her eyes scanned the surroundings, searching for any signs of movement or danger lurking in the shadows. The dim light of the fading sun cast eerie silhouettes, playing tricks on her mind as she navigated the maze of abandoned buildings and debris-strewn roadways. She needed to find a secure building, and made that her mission.

With the infected a mile away, she surveyed the area and spotted a rundown mill. Fixing her gaze on the structure, she inspected the outside before grabbing a stick and pounding on the door. When nothing groaned or moved, she knew it was safe to enter. Inside, the open space sent a spidery sensation down her back, and stairs leading to a second floor were visible.

She moved to the staircase and crept up one step at a time. At the top, she could see multiple doors. With her stick still in hand, she banged on each door as she passed. Pausing at the fifth door, she detected movement inside and decided to leave it closed. She went back downstairs and found a kitchen area.

It appeared safe enough, she thought, so she settled down and dozed off for a much-needed nap.

She awoke to a grunting moan. Startled, she sat up, listening and waiting. Getting off the chair, she went to the door, opened it a little, and caught the unmistakable sound of zombies. Her lungs constricted with fear, forcing her to use her inhaler. She inhaled deeply, pocketing her puffer, and made her way out into the wide-open space.

Looking up, she saw the undead ambling along the hallway, which spurred her into action. She tripped over her untied shoelace, letting out a loud "Oomph" as she fell. To get at her, a ghoul leaned over the banister and plunged to the ground. As it landed, a cloud of dust flew into the air, and the vibration of its landing echoed in Wendy's ears. She got to her feet and took off, just making it to the door with enough time to unbolt it and rush out. It followed.

She ran into a parked vehicle, and in her distress, she had an asthma attack. Grabbing her inhaler, she put it to her lips and inhaled deeply, but nothing came out. She shook it and attempted again, but still no relief came. It was empty, and she was seconds away from being the creature's afternoon snack.

In a panic, Wendy looked over her shoulder. The creature was getting closer with each passing moment, and her options were dwindling faster than a speeding bullet. She dashed around the car, her heart pounding in her chest as she tried the doors. But rusted shut, they offered no escape. With no other choice, she lunged for the trunk, and to her surprise, it swung open with a creak.

Without a second thought, she scrambled inside, her hands trembling as she pulled the cord attached to the trunk's interior, allowing a sliver of light and air to filter through. But before she could catch her breath, the ghoul closed in, its decaying fingers slamming into the car's surface like a battering ram in its mindless pursuit.

As the creature's relentless assault continued, she heard the metallic click of the latch as the luggage compartment was sealed shut, trapping her in darkness. Fear gripped her heart, her asthma attack gaining momentum with every passing second. She kicked the trunk in desperation, but it remained stubbornly fastened. With trembling hands, she tried to pull down the back seats, but they were so rusted together they didn't budge.

Curling into a tight ball, Wendy struggled to regulate her breathing, the outside sounds of the zombie's harsh thumping on the car echoing in her ears.

The air grew thick and suffocating, her chest tightening with each labored breath. With a final gasp, she shut her eyes, succumbing to the overwhelming darkness as her body succumbed to the merciless grip of her asthma attack.

Zombie Movie & TV Trivia Answers: Round 6

1. Zack Snyder.
2. Rick Grimes, portrayed by actor Andrew Lincoln.
3. Bob Balaban.
4. Wade Vogel.
5. Playing baseball.
6. Made her more assertive and capable.
7. The Possession Virus.
8. Kiah Roache-Turner
9. The fast-moving zombies in the film are referred to as "sprinters or "zombie swarms."
10. Tallahassee (played by Woody Harrelson).

Chapter 13

Tony settled into his seat, the faint hum of the airplane engines providing a soothing backdrop to his thoughts. At forty-two years old and flying alone from L.A. to New York, he had hoped for a peaceful journey.

As the flight progressed, Tony's senses were assaulted by an increasing racket of sounds—the drone of conversations, the whir of vents, and the occasional ding of the seatbelt sign. The smell of recycled air mingled with hints of stale pretzels. His taste buds were tingling with the anticipation of his drink. He placed his order and waited. Moments later, the cabin crew served him his whiskey.

He'd gotten through three glasses when he started to observe some odd behaviors. Exchanging quizzical glances with neighboring passengers, he raised an eyebrow as a woman across from him underwent what appeared to be an epileptic seizure. Then he noticed the man kneeling on the floor at the woman's feet and assumed it was some kind of kinky mile-high club thing.

Relaxing back in his seat, he was ready for the entertainment. He pushed the button to get the stewardess and placed an order for another drink. He sipped his refreshment, eager for some much-needed amusement. But he was disappointed when what he believed was about to be hard-core porn turned out to be the complete opposite.

With wide-open eyes, he then noticed the man biting the nearby lady passenger. Unable to make sense of that, he took hold of his glass, gulping down a mouthful of his beverage. He witnessed another traveler convulsing and couldn't ignore the peculiarity any longer. Peering over the top of his seat, he observed a surreal backdrop—fellow passengers engaging in interpretive ape-like movements.

All at once, a commotion erupted a few rows ahead. Screams pierced the air, and panic spread like wildfire as travelers began to realize something was terribly wrong. Tony's heart pounded as he strained to see what was happening, but all he could discern were frantic activity and desperate shouts.

With a rush of energy fueling his every move, his instincts kicked into high gear. Ignoring the disruption unfolding around him, he bolted toward the nearest sanctuary—the bathroom. Inside, he pressed his back to the door, his breaths coming in shallow gasps as he tried to make sense of the madness outside.

Minutes stretched into eternity as he remained, and the silence was broken only by the muffled moans of the afflicted. As the aircraft plunged into severe turbulence, Tony was jolted, tossed about like a ragdoll in a cyclone. His body slammed against the cabin walls, and his head collided with the ceiling with a resounding thud. Stunned and disoriented, he winced as pain shot through his skull.

When the turbulent chaos subsided and the craft steadied, he massaged his throbbing head, his fingertips tracing the tender spot where it had impacted with the unforgiving surface. He summoned the courage to leave the safety of the restroom and return to his seat, determined to finish his drink.

As soon as he opened the door, he was met with pandemonium. People were fighting with one another, running and screaming, but the thing that would stay in his brain forever was the sight of blood. *Zombies. It can't be!* Pushing people out of the way, he fought his way back to his seat, took hold of his beverage, and drank every last drop.

Something grabbed at his back, and he spun around to see decaying fingers reaching for him. Sickened and believing he was drunk, he shoved the arm aside and made his way to the rear of the aircraft.

In his search for a place to avoid getting attacked, Tony's gaze fell upon one of the emergency doors. *Do it!* his mind screamed at him.

No, it's suicide, he argued with himself.

Stop acting like a baby. You'll have a better chance of surviving out there than you will from being eaten. Maybe you could make it to the baggage hold.

He shifted his body and grabbed a half glass of rum and coke from a nearby tray, downing it in one swift gulp before turning to face the door. His hand hovered over the bright red handle.

Turn it. Don't be such a pussy.

With a sinking sensation in his gut, he realized he had stumbled into the heart of a nightmare when he pulled the latch down and it swung sideways with a powerful sucking of air. He found himself on the brink of oblivion, staring into the abyss of the night sky. He believed his life was over, that he was about to be sucked out of the plane.

By pure chance, he was picked up by a whirlwind of a strong swirling draft and hurled onto the wing. Clinging to one of the raised lights with white-knuckled intensity, he latched on by some miracle as the world around him spun in a dizzying blur, his body buffeted by the howling wind.

Tony's digits grew numb with cold, and his muscles ached from the strain of holding on. The icy chill seeped into his bones, a relentless reminder of his unstable position on the edge of oblivion. *A glass of whiskey would warm me up. Yes, if only the stewardess could deliver it to me out here. Oh, who am I kidding, I'm doomed. I should have taken the bottle with me.*

Just as he thought he couldn't hold on any longer, the plane lurched sideways, tilting at an impossible angle. His heart leapt into his throat as he felt himself losing his grip, his body slipping inexorably toward the yawning chasm below.

With a primal scream torn from his lips, Tony plummeted into the darkness, his world reduced to a blur of wind and sky. The ground rushed up to meet him with terrifying speed, a silent witness to his final moments of desperation.

Zombie Movie & TV Trivia: Round 7

1. What is the title of the 2013 romantic zombie comedy film that follows a zombie who becomes more human after consuming brains?
2. In the film *Zombieland: Double Tap*, what nickname does Little Rock give to the pacifist hippie she meets?
3. What is the name of the chemical that reanimates the dead in *The Return of the Living Dead*?
4. In the film *The Dead Don't Die* (2019), what song repeatedly plays on the radio and serves as a harbinger of the impending zombie apocalypse?
5. What is the origin of the virus in the 2002 film *28 Days Later*?
6. Which classic zombie movie features a group of survivors taking shelter in a farmhouse, trying to fend off zombies?
7. Who portrays the character of Miss Justineau, in *The Girl with All the Gifts*?
8. In *Land of the Dead* (2005), what is the name of the fortified city where the elite live while the rest face the zombie horde outside?
9. Which 2006 film, directed by James Gunn, combines zombies with alien parasites taking over a small town?
10. In *Warm Bodies,* what is the name given to the wall protecting the last human enclave from the zombie-infested outside world?

Answers will be found after the next tale.

Chapter 14

Gina, a twenty-eight-year-old woman, was nestled in the comfort of her private cabin aboard the train. Exhausted after working a late shift at the club and doing some nighttime shopping, she had decided to treat herself to a relaxing journey home.

As the rhythmic clatter of the train's wheels filled the compartment, she sensed the weight of her fatigue settling in. Despite her best efforts to stay awake, the gentle sway of the railcar soon lulled her into a drowsy state.

Lost in a haze of exhaustion, she barely registered the distant sounds echoing through the carriage. It wasn't until the commotion erupted into her cabin that she snapped out of her daze.

With a jolt, the door burst open and three zombies flooded inside, their decaying hands reaching out with hunger. Blinking in confusion and still half-asleep, Gina took the peanut butter from her shopping bag, opened it, and offered it to the deadheads. When they showed no interest, she resorted to flinging the jar at them in a desperate attempt to fend them off.

The rotters had one focus, to devour her. Unaffected by her efforts, they continued their relentless advance. Managing to evade their grasping arms, she hovered in the doorframe, uncertain of her next move. All of a sudden, a man and a woman raced past her cabin, dropping items from a backpack in their haste. Seizing one of the dropped objects—a rubber chicken—she brandished it like a weapon, hoping to ward off the infected attackers.

But her valiant attempts were in vain, as the toy proved to be no match for the hungry undead. With a comical squawk, the latex bird flew out of her hand and got tangled in the train's emergency brake cord, inadvertently activating it and bringing the train to a screeching halt.

As the locomotive ground to a standstill, she found herself thrown forward with the force of the sudden stop, hurtling towards the cabin window. With a resounding thud, she collided with the glass and bounced back, landing directly on top of a zombified passenger who had been lurking outside.

The impact knocked the wind out of her, leaving her stunned and disoriented as she struggled to make sense of her surroundings. But before she could gather her wits, the ghoul traveler began to stir. His hungry gaze fixed on her as he reached out to take a bite. In her panic, she spotted the contents of her late-night shopping strewn across the floor. Gina's mind raced for a solution, her eyes scanning the scattered belongings for something useful.

Among the items was a pack of toilet paper, and without a second thought, she seized it and began hurling the rolls at the approaching zombies in an attempt at defense. The soft tissue projectiles fluttered through the air, unfurling in erratic patterns as they sailed in the direction of their targets. The flimsy rolls offered little resistance, disintegrating upon impact and doing little more than briefly obscuring the undead assailants' vision.

She backed up and tripped over something. Turning to see what it was in a last-ditch effort to defend herself, she picked up a discarded, brightly colored umbrella and thrust it toward the zombie's face. In her panic, Gina's heart raced as she fumbled with the handle, the umbrella's unexpected opening knocking her backward with a jolt of surprise.

Faced with limited options, she spotted an opened window and clambered onto the windowsill, convinced that being on top of the train would be her saving grace. As she ventured onto the rooftop, unsteady and doing everything she could to keep from falling, she was met with a surprising sight. She saw a group of people jumping, pointing, and screaming at her, but their voices went unheard and she couldn't make out their warnings.

With the train at a standstill, she found herself teetering on the roof. Her relief was short-lived as the sudden rumble of the engine jolted her back to reality. The locomotive had started up again, lurching forward with unexpected force and sending her tumbling near the edge.

As she scrambled to regain her footing, a low-hanging sign loomed ominously ahead. Despite the frantic alerts of the other survivors, Gina's panicked state left her unable to react in time as the suspended signboard rushed toward her. With a sickening thud, she collided with the billboard and was sent hurtling over the side, plummeting into the waiting arms of a horde of zombies below.

Zombie Movie & TV Trivia Answers: Round 7

1. *Warm Bodies.*
2. Berkeley.
3. Trioxin.
4. *The Dead Don't Die* by Sturgill Simpson.
5. Animal rights activists release infected chimpanzees.
6. *Night of the Living Dead* (1968).
7. Gemma Arterton.
8. Fiddler's Green.
9. *Slither.*
10. The Wall.

Chapter 15

Nestled in the heart of a tranquil suburban neighborhood, Annie's house stood as a symbol of comfort and security, cocooned by the warmth of familiarity. For Annie, the prospect of stepping beyond the threshold into the vastness of the outside world was a daunting nightmare.

The once-beautiful curtains that adorned her windows now became shields against the horrors that lurked outdoors. Locked doors and barricaded entryways were the tangible expressions of her agoraphobic tendencies, providing a deceptive refuge in the face of the undead menace that roamed the streets.

She sat huddled in the corner of her dimly lit living room, her cozy sanctuary now feeling like a prison. Agoraphobia had confined her to these four walls long before the world fell into chaos. Now it seemed the universe had closed in on her.

Her weekly deliveries of supplies, a lifeline that tethered her to the outside, had ceased, leaving her stranded and alone. With each passing day, her stomach churned with hunger, an incessant reminder of her dwindling food reserves. She watched as the meager scraps in her pantry dwindled down to nothing, rationing what little remained with a sense of desperation that bordered on panic.

In the silence of her home, the sound of her belly growling echoed like a thunderous roar. Annie's movements grew sluggish, her once delicate fingers quivering as she scoured the empty shelves for any overlooked morsel. The pangs of starvation gnawed at her insides, a persistent ache that consumed her thoughts and made her weak with deprivation.

She resorted to scavenging for sustenance in the oddest places, picking at crumbs left behind in forgotten corners and gnawing on stale crusts of bread. The comforting rituals of her daily life had been replaced by a single-minded obsession with survival. This drove her to the brink of hopelessness as she fought to stave off the insatiable appetite that threatened to consume her from within.

Annie's despair hit a breaking point as she contemplated her lack of food and the surrounding hordes of zombies. With shaking hands and a racing heart, she mustered the courage to approach the barricaded door, her mind filled with the dread of stepping outside her sanctuary.

As she reached for the handle, panic surged through her veins like a tidal wave, her palms slick with sweat and her breaths coming in short, ragged gasps. The weight of her fear held her like an iron vise, rendering her powerless to move past the threshold.

Unable to confront the terror lurking just beyond her doorstep, Annie sank to the floor, her back pressed against the barricade as she struggled to regain control of her racing thoughts. With each labored breath, she fought off the suffocating grip of panic, her brain awash with a flurry of desperate ideas and half-formed plans.

In the midst of her turmoil, a reckless idea took root in her starved mind—a dangerous gambit born of desperation and necessity. If she couldn't venture out to find food, she would lure one of the zombies to her, dispatch it, and feast on its flesh to sustain herself.

With a newfound sense of purpose, Annie pushed herself to her feet, her resolve hardened by the gnawing ache of hunger and the primal instinct to survive. As she began to formulate her plan, she focused on the rhythmic cadence of her respiration, using deep-breathing exercises to steady her nerves and quell the rising tide of panic.

Though the thought of confronting the undead filled her with dread, she knew that the alternative—slowly wasting away in her prison—was a fate she could not bear to accept. With a firm resoluteness, she steeled herself for the harrowing task ahead, her heart pounding in her chest as she prepared to face the horrors lurking just beyond her barricaded door.

She got to work and bit by bit peeled back an opening from her back door. Using her own flesh as a lure, she stuck her arm through the gap to lure an unsuspecting zombie. When it was close enough, she pushed opened the door, pinning it against the wall. Its flailing arms scared her, but her maddening appetite gave her the strength she needed. Brandishing a hammer, she bashed the ghoul's head in. Once it was double-dead, she dragged it inside and resealed the door. As it lay on the floor, she began filleting it with a butcher knife.

After she'd taken sufficient meat off the thigh, she cooked it up and ate it. During the night, she woke with cramps and a severe stomachache. Rushing to the bathroom and making it in the nick of time, she projectile vomited. When she finished throwing up, she discovered she was still starving. Having expelled what she'd eaten, she needed more. Another meal filled her, and content, she went back to bed.

This time she didn't wake as herself. She realized she'd begun to change. In the quiet desperation of her final moments, surrounded by the echoes of her once-protected abode, she faced the cruel reality of becoming a zombie.

The undead, her perceived external threat, were overshadowed by the silent specter of starvation that loomed from within. The very fear that had confined her again manifested as the insidious grip of hunger, except this time she hungered for a living being. And for the first time in over three decades she was able to leave her house and venture out. This time, she did so to quench her insatiable need to feast on unsuspecting humans.

Zombie Movie & TV Trivia: Round 8

1. Which actor played the role of Columbus in the film *Zombieland* (2009)?
2. In *Dead Snow* (2009), what is the motivation behind the Nazi zombies' attack?
3. Which 2012 film, directed by Juan Carlos Fresnadillo, is a sequel to *28 Days Later*?
4. In the TV series *The Walking Dead*, what is the name of Negan's weapon of choice?
5. What is the name of the protagonist in the 2015 film *Scouts Guide to the Zombie Apocalypse*?
6. In *[*REC]* (2007), what type of building is quarantined by the authorities due to the zombie outbreak?
7. Which 2004 film, directed by Edgar Wright, pays homage to zombie movies while adding a comedic twist?
8. What is the alternative title of *Dead Alive* used in some regions outside of North America?
9. In *Zombieland*, what does Tallahassee search for throughout the film?
10. Which film, directed by Ruben Fleischer, follows a group of survivors in the zombie apocalypse searching for the fabled Pacific Playland?

Answers will be found after the next tale.

Chapter 16

In the dark depths of the ocean, where silence reigns and the world above seems like a distant memory, Howard believed he had found the perfect refuge from the zombie apocalypse—a submarine.

As the ersatz captain of his metallic sanctuary, he felt invincible, surrounded by the impenetrable darkness of the deep blue. Sneaking onboard during the world-ending battle, he had a false sense of security, believing he was safe and that nothing could disrupt his aquatic haven.

He had searched the vessel, ensuring it was empty. Finding no one, he had made himself comfortable in the captain's chair. Reclining the seat and placing his feet up on the control panel, he removed a single cigar he had been saving from his breast pocket. "Ah, the sweet scent of victory." He chuckled, a self-satisfied grin spreading across his face. With the divorce papers signed, he took a deep breath, smiled, and put the tobacco stick in his mouth, breathed in the aroma, and lit it. Sucking down a profound draw, he looked out the porthole and admired the free life of the fish.

He closed his eyes for a moment, wishing he could take the sub below the surface. He opened his eyes to see the room filled with smoke, realizing that without windows he was filling the sub with his fumes. He waved his hands about to try and dissipate the swirling clouds, and failed. Note to self—smoking in a metal tube with no openings is like barbecuing in a closet.

Swinging his feet down, he stood and extinguished the cigar on the tabletop. Leaving it there, he got closer to the viewing port and saw three zombies floating, with their hair whirling eerily around them. He realized that the undead had acquired the unexpected skill of breathing underwater—or maybe they didn't need to breathe, being dead. One of them got nearer, its eyes big and wide, and it was at that moment he realized they had not come from the land above. These ones had to have been down in the water a long time, since they had barnacles stuck to them.

In morbid fascination, he examined them. He saw that they had noticed him as well. With decaying fleshy arms, they reached for the glass, and for a second, he thought they might breach it and get him.

He turned at the stench of something burning to see that some documents near his cigar were ablaze. Reacting quickly, he brushed them off the table and stomped on them until they were out. "This wasn't in the brochure. Submarines, where the only fire drill is when your divorce papers catch fire. Comedy, tragedy, and a dash of irony," he muttered.

He walked out of the room and found the galley. Going straight to the sink, he poured himself a cup of water. The stench of burnt paper wafted toward him, and while he waved his arms to disperse it, he made his way back to see bright orange flames licking the entrance to the command room.

He looked around for a fire extinguisher and remembered the only one he had seen was inside the now-burning room. Not wanting to burn to death but reluctant to exit the submarine, he thought on his feet. Returning to the galley, he found another extinguisher there. Racing off, he blasted the fire until it was out. Coughing and waving his arms about, he couldn't yet enter the control room. Sulking, he made his way to the other end of the sub and stared out a porthole.

With wide eyes, he witnessed marine life acting oddly. Upon further investigation, he realized that the sea life were dead, like the zombies. Decaying schools of fish swam in a frenzy toward the glass he was staring through. They seemed to know he was there, but he couldn't figure out how. Backing up, he watched them peck at the frame of the porthole, their fins flapping back and forth. Their scales damaged and decayed, and some had missing flippers and tails.

Mesmerized by the sight, he made a decision. The fumes from the smoke were not dissipating. He was choking and coughing, and the thought of being invaded by dead aquatic creatures pushed him to exit the sub.

He moved to the hatch and took a peek out. Believing the coast was clear, he climbed out, only to be grabbed at by one of the living dead people. He toppled over and landed on the bow of the submarine, his legs dangling in the water.

He withdrew them when he caught sight of the water being splashed about, and then his eyes fixed on the undead people closing in on him. The situation became worse as he faced the surreal challenge of outsmarting both the surface zombies and the underwater ones.

He dodged the abomination grabbing for him. In doing so, he slipped from the sub and fell headfirst into the abyss. The zombie fish swarmed him like piranhas, and a loud splash reached his ears. He took a quick look and saw that the topside zombie had followed him into the ocean.

His feet were being bitten, and he sensed the drag as he was dragged beneath the surface. While being pulled under, he witnessed the eerie glow of the submarine's interior lights casting a beam into his aqueous tomb. Like a spotlight, it shone on the ones attacking his legs, while his arms were gnawed on by the land biters.

His final thought? Nowhere is safe during a zombie apocalypse, neither land nor sea. With a final soggy gasp of air, his foolishness in letting his guard down sent him to a watery grave.

Zombie Movie & TV Trivia Answers: Round 8

1. Jesse Eisenberg.
2. Seeking revenge for the theft of their treasure.
3. *28 Weeks Later.*
4. Lucille (a baseball bat wrapped in barbed wire).
5. Ben Goudy.
6. An apartment building.
7. *Shaun of the Dead.*
8. The alternative title in some regions outside of North America is *Braindead.*
9. Twinkies.
10. *Zombieland: Double Tap.*

Chapter 17

In the hushed aftermath of a recent heart surgery, Sid lay in an antiseptic hospital room. Anesthesia's lingering fog muddled his senses, creating a surreal dreamscape as the world outside the clinic's windows transformed into a nightmare.

Clad in the standard-issue hospital gown, with monitoring wires trailing behind him like a strange technological tail, he awoke to a health center in disarray. The quiet moans and distant shuffles were inexplicable echoes in the daze of his anesthesia haze. Unbeknownst to him, the zombie apocalypse had taken root, and the once-sterile medical facility had developed into a battleground of the living dead.

Disoriented and weak, he navigated the labyrinthine hallways, his slippers shuffling against the cold linoleum floor. In his groggy condition, the commotion around him seemed like a distorted dream.

While he meandered through the low-lit corridors, he spotted cleaning supplies and a mop. In his foggy-headedness, it reminded him of his job as a janitor. Believing he was at work, he picked up the gear and began to scrub the bloodied remains away.

This impromptu janitorial mission attracted the attention of a zombie nurse who, in her decaying form, was for a moment confused by Sid's peculiar actions. Then his senses slowly returned to him, like pieces of a puzzle clicking into place after a long slumber. The anesthesia haze that had clouded his mind started to dissipate, leaving him in a state of groggy awareness. Blinking against the harsh fluorescent lights of the hospital corridor, he found himself clutching a mop, the coarse fibers of its head scratching at his palm.

A figure lurched towards him from the dim recesses of the hallway. His heart raced as he recognized the familiar shape of a nurse, her once pristine uniform now tattered and stained. But there was something off about her—something unsettling. Her eyes glinted with a hunger that gave Sid goosebumps.

Instinct kicked in, a primal urge to survive. He tightened his grip on the cleaning handle, readying himself for the impending confrontation. With a swift motion, he plunged the sponge into a nearby bucket of dirty water, the liquid sloshing and splattering against the walls.

The zombie caregiver advanced, her outstretched hands reaching for his flesh. Half of his mind screamed warnings of danger, while the other side, still a bit foggy from the lingering effects of anesthesia, urged him to fight back.

Sid swung the mop with all his might, the tassels whipping through the air like a lethal extension of his arm. They struck the undead creature across the face, eliciting a guttural growl as she stumbled backward.

Emboldened by his small victory, he reversed the scrubber, using its shaft to push the zombie nurse away. But she was unyielding, her decayed hands clawing at him with steadfast persistence.

Their movements erupted into a frantic whirlwind of survival, the wooden handle becoming both weapon and shield in the chaotic dance between him and the rotter. As they grappled, Sid's feet skidded on the slick floor, the scent of disinfectant choking the air along with the metallic tang of blood.

In a desperate attempt to gain traction, he kicked off his slippers, the rubber soles flying as he launched himself into the fray. But the deadhead, driven by an insatiable hunger, seemed unfazed by his feeble attempts to fend her off. Despite his efforts, she continued her relentless advance, her decaying hands clawing at him with savage determination.

With a sudden twist, he knocked over the bucket of water, its contents cascading over the tiled floor with a loud splash. Panic surged through him as he struggled to regain his footing, his feet sliding on the slick surface.

In a desperate bid to escape, Sid's eyes locked onto a lone power cord snaking across the ground, its other end attached to a vacuum cleaner close by. With adrenaline pumping through his veins, he lunged towards it, his fingers fumbling with the wet electrical line as he made his unsteady way to a nearby outlet.

With his chest thumping and a pain deep behind his ribs, he hesitated for a moment before plunging the plug into the socket. Instantly, a surge of electricity surged through the wire, coursing through his saturated hand and jolting him with a violent force that rendered him powerless.

The shockwaves convulsed through his body, sending him staggering backward as if struck by a bolt of lightning. In a desperate attempt to regain control, he grabbed at the electrical cable and shocked his dying heart a second time. His muscles spasmed, and his limbs thrashed in all directions.

The zombie nurse, driven by her insatiable hunger, closed in on him with renewed ferocity. Her decaying hands reached out with skeletal fingers, inches away from Sid's trembling form. As she took hold of his flesh, a burst of sparks exploded around the power outlet like fireworks.

With a last spurt of motivation, his body tensed, and he let out a primal scream of defiance. But it was too late. The collision of their bodies sent arcs shooting, the force of the shockwave sending both Sid and the zombie nurse crashing to the ground in a twisted heap.

As darkness enveloped him and his consciousness slipped away into the void, Sid's final thought echoed in his mind. "Such a rookie mistake for a novice cleaner."

Zombie Movie & TV Trivia: Round 9

1. Where did *World War Z* take place?
2. Who directed the 2009 film *Zombieland*?
3. What are the weakness of the zombies in *Train to Busan*?
4. Which 2017 film, directed by Sang-ho Yeon, is an animated prequel to *Train to Busan*?
5. What is the term used for the zombies in the film *28 Days Later* to emphasize their extreme aggression?
6. In the 2013 film *Warm Bodies,* what item does R collect as a hobby?
7. Which 2016 film, directed by Colm McCarthy, features a young girl with a unique perspective on the zombie apocalypse?
8. What is the name of the virus in the *Resident Evil* film series that turns humans into zombies?
9. In *Shaun of the Dead,* what is the name of the pub that serves as the survivors' primary refuge?
10. Who plays the character Tallahassee in the film *Zombieland: Double Tap*?

Answers will be found after the next tale.

Chapter 18

In the sterile confines of the maternity ward, where the scent of antiseptic heralds the promise of new life, Paula, nine months pregnant with high blood pressure, found herself thrust into an unforeseen vortex of survival. Little had she known that her journey through childbirth would take such an unpredictable turn, as the echoes of the approaching undead reached her ears.

The once-bustling birthing suite, alive with the anticipation of newborn cries, had now transformed into a nightmarish stage where life and death engaged in a whirlwind of unexpected scenarios. She was already grappling with the pains of labor, and was about to face an additional challenge—one that no delivery class could have prepared her for.

As chaos unfolded and the hospital corridors filled with peculiar sounds, Paula's contractions seemed to sync with the rhythmic approach of the zombies. The flickering incandescent lights overhead cast an eerie glow on the scene, turning the once-bustling maternity ward into a surreal mismatched spectacle.

Not wanting to stick around and be part of the unconventional drama, she spied a closet and wobbled to it, while holding tightly to her belly. The closet door's knob had some kind of foul goop on it, but she turned it anyway. Inside the closet, she crumbled to the floor, bent her knees, and heaved out long breaths.

In the midst of labor now, she vocalized her pains. Her body contorted in agony within the cramped confines of the storage space, her hands gripping the nearby shelves with a vise-like grip. Each contraction ripped through her like a flood, rendering her breathless and trembling. She bit down hard on her lip, stifling the urge to cry out as the pain threatened to overwhelm her.

Outside, the thunderous thuds and obstinate scratches of the infected echoed through the thin walls, their monstrous moans mingling with her agonized cries. Every reverberation was a chilling reminder of the imminent peril she faced. Her heart raced, and a ringing sensation filled her ears.

Fear gripped her as she imagined the decaying hands clawing at the door, driven by the primal instinct to reach the source of the sounds. Yet, with no other options, she forced herself to block out the racket of the undead. She channeled all her focus and strength into the singular task of birthing her child.

She squeezed her eyes shut, blocking everything out around her as she concentrated on the rhythmic pattern of her breathing. With each exhale, she pushed down the dread, channeling all her energy into the single goal of bringing her offspring into the world.

The minutes stretched into an eternity as she endured the harrowing ordeal, the sounds of the deadheads growing louder with every passing moment. But she refused to let them distract her and allow them to break her resolve.

And then, with one final, gut-wrenching push, a surge of relief washed over her as the baby slipped from her body, crying out in protest at the sudden change in environment. Tears of joy and exhaustion streamed down her cheeks as she cradled her newborn in her arms. The fear and pain of the past seven hours melted away in an instant.

In that moment, as she gazed down at the tiny, fragile life she had birthed, she was overwhelmed with the parental need to keep her child safe from the horrors that lurked outside their flimsy sanctuary. Hallucinations set in, accompanied by fatigue. Initially, she only saw what she wanted to see. When she allowed her mind to clear, she discovered that her son wasn't as cute as her initial perception had led her to believe.

She thought at first that he must have been stillborn. However, with his decaying, decomposing flesh and dark black eyes, his features bore those of the undead. Wondering how this could have happened, she noticed she still had doorknob goop on her hand and a paper cut on her finger. Maybe some kind of zombie essence in that goop had gotten into her wound and been transported to the baby.

He was suckling in a frenzy on another of her fingers, to the point it broke the skin. Ignoring the pain and accepting what he was, she cradled him until he grew more agitated. Then, fearing for her life, she tucked him into a corner of the closet. Would she also become a zombie?

Her lips cracked and an undeniable thirst hit her hard. With the zombie baby crying with haunting moans, she backed up in distress, knocking over cleaning equipment in the cramped space. One of the bottles rolled to her feet.

Thirsty and exhausted from giving birth, she reached for what she assumed was a bottle of water in the semi-dark room, her fingers closing around the cold, round shape. Without a moment's hesitation, she twisted off the cap and tilted it to her lips, parched and desperate for hydration after the ordeal of childbirth. But as the liquid hit her tongue, a wave of revulsion washed over her. The unmistakable taste of acrid chemicals flooded her senses, sending alarm bells ringing in her mind.

In that instant, she realized her grave mistake. She didn't grab a bottle of water, but instead ingested a toxic chemical. Horror and terror gripped her as she struggled to comprehend the severity of her error. With each passing second, the corrosive solution burned its way down her throat, leaving a trail of destruction in its wake.

As the realization sank in, she doubled over in agony, clutching her chest as if trying to physically wrench out the poison coursing through her veins. But it was futile. The damage was done, and her body succumbed to the lethal effects of the substance she had mistakenly drunk in her desperate thirst.

In her final moments, amidst the searing pain and overwhelming despair, she weakly scanned the label on the bottle now lying beside her, barely able to make out the words through tear-blurred eyes. 'Industrial Grade Hydrochloric Acid,' it read, as if mocking her tragic mishap. And with that bitter revelation, she breathed her last breath.

Zombie Movie & TV Trivia Answers: Round 9

1. Ruben Fleischer.
2. Philadelphia.
3. The zombies have poor vision.
4. Seoul Station.
5. Rage Virus.
6. Vinyl records.
7. *The Girl with All the Gifts.*
8. T-Virus.
9. The Winchester.
10. Woody Harrelson.

Chapter 19

Aboard a small rental yacht amidst the boundless ocean, Nelson and his mate Aaron set out for what was intended to be a tranquil fishing excursion. However, their journey quickly spiraled into a harrowing ordeal when Aaron suddenly collapsed, writhing in pain as he clutched his chest. Despite Nelson's frantic efforts to assist, including administering CPR for twenty minutes, his friend succumbed to a heart attack.

Unbeknownst to him, Aaron's passing triggered the awakening of a dormant zombie virus within his body, turning him into a voracious undead entity. Faced with imminent danger, Nelson erected a wooden barricade to fend off the now-zombified Aaron. But Aaron was the sailor and Nelson didn't know how to navigate. The hours stretched into agonizing days as he grappled with the terrifying truth of his predicament. He was lost at sea.

As his meager supplies dwindled and desperation gnawed at his sanity, Nelson's hopes were dealt another blow when the boat's motor sputtered and died, the fuel reserves exhausted. With no means of propulsion, his only option was to try to erect the sails in a frantic attempt to catch the wind and steer towards dry land, wherever that was.

But fate seemed determined to thwart him at every turn. The sea remained eerily calm, the sailcloth hanging limp and useless in the stagnant air. Trapped in a nightmarish limbo, he grappled with a gnawing sense of helplessness as he stared out at the endless expanse of saltwater stretching in all directions.

With each elapsing day, his predicament grew increasingly dire. Without access to fresh water and dwindling food supplies, he faced an impossible choice. Should he remain adrift in the hopes of a chance encounter with a passing ship, or risk swimming in the unknown expanse of the ocean in search of land?

As hunger gnawed at his stomach and thirst parched his throat, his resolve wavered. The once-clear line between survival and surrender blurred, and he found himself teetering on the precipice of madness. His mood was further tested by his turned friend, whose groaning and snapping mouth disturbing him. He thought about eating him, then decided it was a dumb idea. The barricade he had erected would hold tight, he was certain of it. What he wasn't sure of was how he would survive.

In a fit of frustration, he grabbed a nearby fishing rod and cast it into the water, hoping against hope for a stroke of luck. But without bait, his efforts were futile. The line remained untouched and lifeless, mocking his desperation. He walked over to the barrier with one thing on his mind, to chat.

"So, what's it like being a zombie?" he quipped, receiving an exaggerated grunt in reply.

"I see. Well then, I suppose now's the best time to come clean. I slept with your wife," he continued, staring at the corpse and waiting for a response. When none came, he added, "You are boring," accompanied by more grunts from the ghoul.

"Wanna see a trick?" he asked, undeterred. More groans followed. "I knew you would. Well, just keep your eyes on me," he said, climbing onto the railings and holding one leg up as he hopped along it. "I bet you can't do that," he taunted, and was met with more moans in reply.

All of a sudden, he lost his footing. With a sickening thud, he landed squarely on his nuts. Agony shot through his body like lightning as he clutched his groin, writhing in excruciating pain. As he struggled to regain his composure, his unsteady movements propelled him sideways, sending him crashing to the deck.

Still clutching his throbbing manhood, he scrambled to his feet and faced the wooden planks. "This is all your fault! All of it. If you hadn't had a stupid heart attack, I wouldn't be facing this crap," he shouted in frustration, hitting the beam so hard that it broke his wrist. "Now look what you did!" he exclaimed, met with more groans.

Frustrated, he sat on a box and wrapped his injured hand with his tee shirt. An idea struck him like a bolt of lightning, and he raced off to the control room. He snatched the flare gun, though knowing deep down that no savior would likely come to his aid. With the weapon gripped tightly, he dashed back to where his zombie friend, Aaron, was.

Pointing the muzzle at him, Nelson's voice grew louder. "I ought to blow your brains out!" he threatened. He was greeted with more groans. "Do you know any other sounds besides those stupid moans?" he mocked, waving the firearm around in frustration. "Come on, wank stain, say something!"

Met with only grunts in response, his annoyance boiled over. He shifted his body so he was now standing in front of the planks, and slipped his good hand through the gap and wriggled it about. "Hungry?" he taunted, withdrawing his hand just as the undead one lunged for it. "Come on, bitch, eat me!" he scoffed, repeating the act.

Then, with a sudden shift in mood, he climbed back onto the railings, positioning himself above the barrier where the infected one lurked. The flare was now pointed downward, aimed at the rotter below. He continued his taunts, swinging his legs back and forth to catch Aaron's attention. "You want me, don't you?" he jeered, a loud grumble emanating from the pit.

"Too bad you can't reach me," he laughed, playing with the gun as if it were a toy. But then a somber realization washed over him, and his mood shifted once more. "This is it, it's now or never. Any last words?" he asked, met only with grunts from the deadhead.

"Of course, why would I ever think you had the capacity to actually speak? You're nothing but a monster," he spat, standing up on the railings. But in his moment of hubris, he lost his balance, his finger squeezing the trigger as he fell. The flare gun discharged and shot him in the thigh with a deafening bang. With a busted wrist and a bleeding wound, he knew it would only be a matter of time before he succumbed to his injuries.

"Great, now I'm gonna die, thanks to you!" he muttered, his words tinged with resentment towards his former friend who had succumbed to the zombie virus. His eyes fixed on the makeshift barricade of timber that separated him from Aaron, realizing the grim reality of his situation. "I guess I'll see you in the afterlife, brother. For the record, I didn't really sleep with your wife," he whispered, knowing that his fate was sealed.

Zombie Movie & TV Trivia: Round 10

1. What is the title of the 1986 film directed by Fred Dekker, in which a group of kids battles zombies in their neighborhood?
2. In *Dead Snow*, what is the origin of the Nazi zombies?
3. Which 2016 film, directed by Sang-ho Yeon, is set on a train and explores themes of class struggle during a zombie outbreak?
4. What was the virus' name in the zombie apocalypse in the film *Maggie* (2015)?
5. Which 2012 film, directed by Andrew Currie, combines the zombie genre with a dark comedy set in a small town?
6. In *Dawn of the Dead* (2004), what does the character Andy use to communicate with the survivors in the shopping mall?
7. Who played the role of Selena, a survivor in *28 Days Later*?
8. Where did the zombie battle take place in the movie *Goal of the Dead*?
9. In *Land of the Dead* (2005), what is the nickname given to the gas station attendant zombie who becomes self-aware?
10. What unique method do the zombies use to spread the infection in *Pontypool* (2009)?

Answers will be found after the next tale.

Chapter 20

It was an ordinary day for twenty-eight-year-old Terry as he manned the toll booth, diligently collecting cash from cars passing on the highway. The morning had started like any other. After completing a Christmas shopping spree, he had made his way to his job. Routine was key in his line of work, and he let himself in as he always did, settling into his chair with a sense of familiarity.

But the tranquility of the day was shattered when a car crashed into the railings nearby. As he moved to exit his station and offer assistance, he froze in horror as he watched the driver lurch out of the vehicle and attack the car's other passenger. The realization hit him like a ton of bricks—the man was a zombie. And as Terry's gaze swept across the highway, he recognized that he was being surrounded by more crashes, more screams, and more zombies.

Panic gripped him as he struggled to comprehend the magnitude of the situation unfolding before him. He was trapped within the tollgate and isolated from the outside world, with no means of escape. The air inside was suffocating, the heat unbearable as sweat poured down his back and drenched his shirt.

In the midst of his fear and worry, his mind raced, searching for a way out. Contemplating a getaway plan, he knew he had to act fast. But his thoughts were muddled, clouded by the overwhelming sense of dread that threatened to consume him.

Rummaging through the gifts he had purchased earlier that morning, he searched for something, anything, that could help him survive. And then he found something—nestled among the other presents, a Nerf gun and a super-powered water blaster. But picking those items up sent a wave of misery through his veins. He wondered if his two sons would be okay. Had they escaped turning into the undead? Had his wife turned? His thoughts motivated him, and he decided he had to make it home—to be the father, and the protective husband.

With renewed vigor, he put things in motion, loading foam bullets into the Nerf gun's magazine and strapping it to his chest like Rambo. Then he filled the reservoir of the water blaster with the two bottles of champagne he had bought for his mother-in-law, to use them as improvised liquid ammunition.

Armed and ready, he steeled himself for what lay ahead. The toll booth door creaked open as he stepped out onto the highway, the sound of his pounding heart echoing in his ears. The battle for survival had begun, and he was geared up to fight.

As he faced the onslaught of flesh eaters, he knew that this would be a Christmas like no other. With his Nerf gun in his hand and the champagne-loaded water gun primed, he was determined to make it through alive. With a surge of energy he unleashed a barrage of foam darts and bubbly blasts, fighting with all his might against the undead horde.

To his dismay, his plastic toy-weapons seemed to have little effect on the zombie assailants. They didn't falter, and they didn't stumble. Instead, they continued their slow, inexorable march toward him, their persistent pursuit unfazed by his desperate attempts at defense.

As he trudged along the unforgiving asphalt of the highway, beads of sweat mingled with the grime on his furrowed brow, his heart drumming a frantic rhythm in his chest. Each step felt like a laborious feat, weighed down by the impending doom that lurked around every corner. He had expended his last Nerf bullets with fervent desperation, the playful whiz of foam projectiles now replaced by a hollow silence. The once-refreshing spritzes from his water blaster had transformed into feeble spurts of champagne, a mocking reminder of his dwindling defenses against the encroaching horde of zombies.

He spotted a construction site that loomed like a distant oasis in a desert of despair. Its skeletal frames and towering cranes cast long shadows that danced in the fading light of the setting sun. With the guttural moans of the undead echoing ominously in his ears and each breath tearing through his lungs like a blade, his muscles screamed in protest as he pushed his weary body beyond its limits.

When he reached the construction area, his eyes widened in frantic urgency as he scanned the cluttered landscape for a lifeline in the middle of the mayhem. Cones lay strewn across the ground, their vibrant hues dulled by the pall of impending doom that hung in the atmosphere. Tools of destruction littered the place like discarded relics of a forgotten civilization—jackhammers, chainsaws, and heavy-duty drills beckoning to him with a siren's call of salvation.

With a surge of drive, he lunged towards the nearest jackhammer, his quivering hands fumbling for purchase among the advancing walking dead. The cold steel of the hammer's shaft sent a jolt of anticipation coursing through his veins, its weight a reassuring anchor amidst the storm of uncertainty that raged within him.

As Terry's trembling fingers closed around the handle, a burst of primal fear shot through his body like a lightning bolt, electrifying every nerve and sinew with an unrelenting intensity. He flicked the switch, unleashing the full force of the jackhammer's power in a deafening cacophony of mechanical fury.

The impact was immediate and overwhelming. The ground quaked beneath his feet as the jackhammer roared to life, its thunderous vibrations reverberating through his entire being like an internal earthquake. His teeth rattled in his skull, his bones vibrating with a raw fierceness that threatened to tear him apart from the inside out.

With a sickening lurch, Terry felt his body torn asunder by the merciless energy of the hammer's recoil. His limbs thrashed about as he was propelled backward into the waiting embrace of the encroaching horde. Dazed and disoriented, he sprawled on the unforgiving asphalt, his senses reeling from the onslaught of disorder that engulfed him.

And as the relentless swarm closed in around him, he could do nothing but watch in helpless horror as the undead descended upon him in a frenzied uproar of gnashing teeth and grasping hands. The end came fast, and Terry's world faded into darkness.

Zombie Movie & TV Trivia Answers: Round 10

1. *Night of the Creeps.*
2. A curse placed on the gold they stole.
3. *Train to Busan.*
4. Necroambulist Virus.
5. Fido.
6. Written messages on a whiteboard.
7. Naomie Harris.
8. The stadium.
9. Big Daddy.
10. The infection is spread through the English language itself, with certain words and phrases acting as triggers for violent and irrational behavior.

Chapter 21

Henry, an intrepid hiker with a passion for conquering the great outdoors, embarked on a hiking trail surrounded by the beauty of untouched nature. As he trekked deeper into the center of the forest, the once serene ambiance gave way to an eerie stillness. The rustling of leaves and the distant calls of wildlife seemed to fade into the background, replaced by an unsettling quiet that sent shivers down his spine.

All of a sudden, the tranquility was shattered by the guttural groans of the undead. Henry froze in his tracks, his heart pounding in his chest as he scanned the surrounding trees for any sign of movement. His senses were on high alert, every nerve tingling with apprehension as he strained to catch a glimpse of the approaching danger.

And then he saw them—a group of figures staggering through the woods, their movements disjointed and unnatural. Henry's breath caught in his throat as he realized they were not the ordinary backpackers he had expected to encounter. These were something else entirely, their vacant eyes and slack-jawed expressions revealing their true nature as the undead.

Panic surged through his veins as he watched the zombie hikers draw closer, their moans growing louder with each passing second. He knew he had to act fast if he wanted to escape their grasp, but fear rooted him to the spot, rendering him unable to move.

With a sudden burst of energy, Henry tore away from the scene, his footsteps echoing loudly in the silent forest. He sprinted blindly through the underbrush, branches whipping against his skin as he fought to put as much distance between himself and the approaching horde as possible.

Just as he thought he had eluded them, a hand shot out from the shadows. It grabbed hold of his ankle with a vise-like grip. He stumbled, his heart leaping into his throat as he struggled to break free from the undead assailant's grasp.

In a frantic struggle, he kicked out wildly, his hiking boots connecting with something soft and yielding underfoot. With a sickening squelch, the zombie hiker released its clutch, its rotted flesh no match for the force of Henry's blow.

As he fled, he took a chance to peer over his shoulder. Not watching where he was going, he ran right into a tree.

The impact knocked him to the ground. He couldn't see for a second. As his sight returned, he sprang to his feet, ready to take off. But his shoelace tripped him up, and he went careening down a small bank. He landed in a patch of poison ivy, to which he was highly allergic. In a mad rush to scratch the stinging itch that was fast spreading, he backed into a shrub. Coming from the bush, an almighty roar hit his ears, and the rustling of leaves revealed an imposing bear. He gazed at the saliva spewing from its maw as he withdrew himself.

The impossible irritation he was experiencing caused him to drop to the ground, just as one of the rotters reached out to grab him. Henry took advantage of the situation by rolling across the terrain—and right into the lower limbs of another infected one. He scrambled out of the way again, only to end up back at the feet of the grizzly. It stood on its hind legs and let out a roar, the sound piercing the air.

Now caught in the crossfire between the undead and a wild beast, his options dwindled. In a moment of desperate ingenuity, he attempted to use his hiking poles as makeshift weapons against both sets of attackers, resulting in a clumsy and ineffective defense. The rapid spread of hives on his face and exposed back made him dance in agony, resembling someone treading on hot coals.

Feeling trapped in the middle of the rotters and the grizzly, Henry's thoughts raced for a solution. With a sudden surge of irrational bravery, he darted through the legs of the bear, scrambling onto its back in a misguided attempt to utilize it as a shield from the zombies. He convinced his mind that it was the only path to stay alive. The animal, having none of it, deliberately fell backward with a forceful motion to rid itself of the unwanted rider.

As Henry crashed to the ground, pinned beneath the weight of the bruin, he found himself in an even worse predicament. The impact had knocked the wind out of him, leaving him vulnerable and exposed. Before he could even try to move, the grizzly, startled by his intrusion, shifted its mass and crushed him further below its massive bulk.

With a sudden shift, the mammal turned around to face him, its claws swiping him across his chest. Incapable of moving, he was consumed by the intense pressure, with no choice but to scream. The zombies seized the opportunity and closed in on him. Henry's shrieks echoed, and the forest converted into a grim amphitheater of his demise.

In the aftermath, the satisfied bear lumbered back into the wilderness, leaving behind a chilling scene of carnage. Henry's remains became a gruesome feast for scavengers, a tragic end to what was meant to be a picturesque hiking adventure.

Zombie Movie & TV Trivia: Round 11

1. In the film *Shaun of the Dead,* what does Shaun do for a living?
2. Which 2016 South Korean zombie film involves characters on a train fighting against an infected horde?
3. In *Zombieland,* what is Columbus' real name before he adopts the rule-based moniker?
4. Who directed the 2013 romantic zombie comedy film *Warm Bodies*?
5. What is Negan's full name in *The Walking Dead* comics and television series?
6. Which 1985 film, directed by Dan O'Bannon, revolves around a group of medical supply warehouse workers dealing with reanimated cadavers?
7. What is the name of the small town in which the characters of *Scouts Guide to the Zombie Apocalypse* try to survive?
8. Which 2012 film, directed by Marc Forster, explores a global zombie pandemic and its impact on different countries?
9. What is the title of the 1990 remake of George A. Romero's *Night of the Living Dead*?
10. In *Dead Snow,* what is the primary motivation behind the Nazi zombies' attack?

Answers will be found after the next tale.

Chapter 22

Bob the pool cleaner was a man of paradoxes. Despite his job of maintaining the pristine beauty of swimming pools, he had a secret–he couldn't swim to save his life, quite literally. His seemingly incongruous fear of water stemmed from a childhood trauma that had left an indelible mark on his psyche.

As a young boy, he had accompanied his family on a summer vacation to a picturesque riverside cabin. Excited at the prospect of frolicking in the cool, inviting waters of the river, he had eagerly donned his bathing trunks and rushed towards the water's edge.

However, what began as a carefree day of aquatic adventure quickly turned into a nightmare. Buoyed by his youthful exuberance and a false sense of confidence, he had ventured too far from shore, oblivious to the treacherous currents lurking beneath the depths.

Suddenly, without warning, he found himself engulfed in the chilly embrace of the river's unforgiving currents. Panic seized him as he thrashed about in the water, desperately gasping for air as he struggled to keep his head above the surface.

In that moment of terror, he experienced a sensation of helplessness unlike anything he had known. The river, once a symbol of carefree childhood joy, had become a menacing abyss threatening to swallow him whole.

Fortunately, he was eventually rescued by a vigilant lifeguard who had spotted his flailing form from the shore. Wheezing for breath and trembling with fear, he was pulled from the water's grasp and deposited onto the safety of the shore. The trauma of his near-drowning experience disabled him from learning to swim. It didn't deter him from attending summer vacations or beach barbeques, but it did prevent him from ever taking a dip again.

On what appeared like just another ordinary day, with the sun gleaming and the sky a perfect blue canvas, he found himself at the lavish pool of a wealthy household. What he failed to detect was the unstoppable zombie apocalypse, ready to turn his day from cleaning to screaming. He mistook the guttural sounds for those of the homeowner's teenage son listening to a rock band.

As the undead descended upon the once-tranquil neighborhood, the affluent family Bob was hired to clean morphed into the living dead. They eyed him less like their savior and more like their next meal. And thus his aquatic adventure began.

Armed with nothing but his servicing tools and a cocktail of chemicals, he valiantly attempted to fend off the approaching rotters. The leaf scooper became his shield, and the pole his trusty lance of pool-cleaning justice. It was like a bad movie, only this time he was the unlikely hero fighting a horde of rotting corpses.

With the determination of a man facing a clogged filter, he unleashed chlorine tablets like they were mini hand grenades, creating a fizzing barrier of undead deterrence. The flesh eaters, now a threat to his safety, floundered around the poolside in a clumsy attempt to reach him. Their bodies were penetrated by the pills, causing them to fizz up like shaken soda cans and become covered in frothy foam as they stumbled with purpose.

To his surprise, his unconventional defense strategy worked, sending the walking dead back in awkward, hissing retreats. Some fell into the water with a comical splash, while others fumbled, unsure of their newfound effervescent froth.

But in a twist of tragic irony, Bob's downfall came not from the reanimated, but from the pool itself. In his frantic effort to maintain his chlorine-fueled protection, he accidentally spilled the slippery chemical concoction onto the deck, turning it into a temporary slip 'n slide of doom.

With the grace of a frog trying to balance a beach ball, he slid across the pool's rim, unaware of the treacherous puddle he had created. And just like that, with a resounding splat that would make even the most elegant swan jealous, he executed an involuntary, ungraceful, and painful split.

With his legs wide apart, he teetered on the edge, swaying to keep from falling. Then he sensed it, a sneeze building fast that he couldn't stop. He hurled overboard and into the water. With helicopter arms and a less-than-sophisticated belly flop, he found himself face-down with the biters in the water.

As he sank beneath the surface, his watery calamity reached its submerged conclusion.

In the interim, the undead, perhaps perplexed by the unexpected turn of events, continued their awkward poolside parade, now smothered in foam, leaving poor Bob to his aqueous fate.

Zombie Movie & TV Trivia Answers: Round 11

1. He works at an electronics store.
2. *Train to Busan.*
3. Mike.
4. Jonathan Levine.
5. Negan Smith.
6. *The Return of the Living Dead.*
7. Deerfield.
8. *World War Z.*
9. *Night of the Living Dead.*
10. Seeking revenge for the theft of their treasure.

Chapter 23

Claire had trained for months, pushing herself through grueling workouts and early morning runs to prepare for the marathon. She was determined to cross that finish line, to feel the rush of accomplishment that came with completing such a daunting challenge. As the starting gun fired, she surged forward with the crowd, her heart pounding with excitement and anticipation.

The first few miles of the race passed in a blur of fervor and perseverance. She focused on maintaining her pace, blocking out the fatigue creeping into her muscles. But as she rounded a corner into the next stretch of the course, she noticed something was off.

The streets that had been bustling with cheering spectators and fellow runners were now emptying as everyone fled. Confusion flickered across Claire's face as she scanned her surroundings, trying to make sense of the sudden change. And then she saw them—figures stumbling and lurching towards her with vacant eyes and outstretched arms.

Panic surged through her veins as she realized what was happening. The marathon had turned into a nightmare. Without hesitating, she veered off the main road, seeking an escape route. That's when she spotted it—a lone skateboard lying abandoned on the sidewalk.

With no other options in sight, Claire made a split-second decision and lunged for the wheeled board. As she pushed off and gained speed, a surge of fear pulsed through her. For a moment, it felt like she was flying, with the wind whipping through her hair as she navigated the empty streets.

But then reality crashed back in as she approached the next corner. The road ahead was cracked and uneven, littered with debris from the upheaval unfolding around her.

As she rounded the bend, her skateboard hit a pothole with a jolt that sent her soaring. Time appeared to slow as she tumbled through the air, the ground rushing up to meet her with a sickening thud. Pain shot through her limbs as she skidded across the pavement, her momentum coming to a halt in a crumpled heap.

Groaning, she got up, wincing as she assessed the damage. Scrapes and bruises covered her arms and legs, but miraculously, nothing seemed to be broken. Ignoring the protests of her battered body, she forced herself to stand, her eyes scanning the surroundings for any indication of danger.

To her relief, the zombies had lost interest in her, their attention now focused on a group of survivors huddled nearby. With grim willpower, she limped away from the scene, her mind racing with thoughts of escape.

Hours passed as she navigated the deserted streets, her footsteps echoing in the eerie silence. She scavenged for supplies, searching abandoned buildings for any sign of food or shelter. With each passing moment, the reality of her situation sank in—she was alone in a world overrun by the undead, with no way of knowing if help would ever come.

But she refused to give up hope. She clung to the belief that somewhere out there, other survivors were fighting to stay alive, just like her. And until she found them, she would do whatever it took to survive.

Months passed after Claire's daring escape from the zombie horde. She became a rookie survivalist, honing her skills in scavenging and fending off the occasional infected straggler. But despite her newfound expertise in navigating the post-apocalyptic world, she couldn't shake the feeling of loneliness that weighed heavily on her heart.

One day, as she scoured a supermarket for supplies, she stumbled upon a shelf stocked with cans of expired SpaghettiOs. Hungry and desperate, she ignored the expiration dates and decided to indulge in a can of long-forgotten comfort food on the spot.

With a growling stomach, she pried open the can and took a hesitant bite. But as soon as the cold, slimy noodles coated in congealed tomato sauce touched her tongue, she gagged in disgust. The taste was revolting, a foul concoction of rancid paste and mushy pasta.

In a fit of frustration, she hurled the can across the room, where it collided with a stack of metal shelves. With a deafening crash, the rack came tumbling down, sending a cascade of debris raining down upon her. She coughed and sneezed, and when the dust settled she picked up another can and flung it to the other side of the room. Without realizing it, all the commotion she was making was drawing the dead closer to her.

As the zombie horde closed in on the supermarket, she glanced towards the back exit, knowing she could slip away to safety. But instead of running away, a strange compulsion took hold of her. With trembling hands, she began to hurl the tinned goods at the advancing walkers, each throw more desperate than the last.

"Buddy, you're a boy, make a big noise," she belted out, while stomping her feet in tune to the music, creating a rhythmic beat that echoed through the aisles. The deadheads, unfazed by her attack, continued to advance, drawn by the ruckus she was making and the scent of fresh meat.

"We will, we will, rock you," she carried on, her vocal cords growing louder and more frantic with every passing minute as she persisted in flinging the canned goods. Despite knowing she could escape, she felt a strange sense of defiance wash over her. She was tired of running of living in fear. In this moment, she chose to stand her ground, even if it meant her death.

When the first zombie reached her, her tone faltered, her song cut short by the inevitable. With a gut-wrenching scream, she was bitten and a wave of regret hit her.

In her last moments, her mind raced with disbelief. She knew she could have outrun them, outmaneuvered them—but for some inexplicable reason, she chose to stay and sing to them instead.

As the realization washed over her, her heart sank with remorse. Why did she do that? Why did she throw away her chance for survival in exchange for a moment of frivolity?

In the climax, as the rotters tore into her skin, her ultimate epiphany dawned upon her. She just wanted to have some fun, to cling to a fleeting sense of normalcy in the chaos of the end of the world. But now, it was too late.

With her final breath, Claire's repentance echoed through the desolate aisles of the supermarket. She would be forever remembered by any who witnessed her end as the survivor who chose to stay and sing to the zombies.

Zombie Movie & TV Trivia: Round 12

1. Which actor played the lead role in the 2007 horror-comedy film *Fido,* where a boy befriends a zombie?
2. In the film *Maggie* (2015), what is the name of the character played by Arnold Schwarzenegger, who cares for his infected daughter?
3. What is the nickname given to the intelligent zombie in George A. Romero's *Land of the Dead* (2005)?
4. Which 2012 film, directed by Andrew Currie, features a post-apocalyptic world where zombies are used as a domestic workforce?
5. What is the objective of the main characters in *The Battery* (2012) during the zombie apocalypse?
6. Who directed the 1985 horror-comedy film *Return of the Living Dead*?
7. In *I Am Legend,* what is the name of the protagonist and virologist played by Will Smith?
8. Which 2013 film features a unique twist on the zombie genre by portraying zombies as a metaphor for a deteriorating marriage?
9. What is the name of the virus that causes the zombie apocalypse in the 2013 film *World War Z*?
10. In *Zombieland: Double Tap,* what is the nickname given to the pacifist hippie played by Avan Jogia?

Answers will be found after the next tale.

Chapter 24

Rachel, a seasoned mountaineer at the age of thirty, clung to the rugged cliff face alongside her lifelong friend and climbing partner, Kiki. The sheer magnitude of the cliff's height—an impressive 1500 feet—was both exhilarating and daunting as they ascended, their fingers gripping onto the cold, weathered rock.

Despite the perilous terrain, they were in high spirits. Their laughter echoed through the mountainous landscape as they exchanged jokes and shared dreams of the celebrations awaiting them once they conquered the summit. The sun cast a warm glow on their faces as they continued their climb, each foothold and handhold bringing them closer to their goal.

Then, without warning, the tranquility of their ascent shattered as a sudden noise pierced the air. Rachel's heart skipped a beat, and she instinctively glanced upward, her stare locking onto a massive boulder that had become dislodged from above. Time seemed to slow as the chunk of stone plummeted downward, its path aimed directly at her friend.

With a sickening thud, the rock struck Kiki with brutal force, shattering the peaceful serenity of their mountaineering. Rachel's breath caught in her throat as she stared in disbelief, horror washing over her as her dear friend's life was abruptly extinguished.

But the dread didn't end there. As her stunned gaze remained fixed on her friend's motionless form, a surreal transformation unfolded before her eyes. Kiki's body convulsed unnaturally, her limbs contorting at twisted angles within her harness, her eyes vacant and devoid of life. In that moment, her world turned upside down as she realized that her friend had become one of the undead.

A wave of fear and uncertainty washed over Rachel as she grappled with the unreal nightmare unfolding in front of her. Her mind raced with disbelief, struggling to comprehend the impossible scenario that had occurred in mere moments.

With Kiki now transformed into a zombie and some essential climbing gear lost with her, Rachel found herself in a precarious situation. The weight of her predicament pressed down on her as she clung to the cliff face, her options dwindling with each passing second.

Anguish gripped her as she surveyed her surroundings, her senses heightened in the face of imminent danger. The jagged rocks loomed ominously around her, casting long shadows in the fading light of day. The wind whipped against her face, carrying with it the faint scent of pine and earth.

Despite her mounting fear, she refused to succumb to despair. With a will to keep going, she swung from her position, attempting to reach Kiki's backpack dangling just out of reach. Her muscles strained with effort as she extended her hand, fingers grasping for the lifeline that could mean the difference between life and death.

Rachel's desperate attempt fell short as she missed the bag by mere inches. Her heart sank with frustration as she realized the pointlessness of her efforts, the harsh reality of her situation sinking in with each passing moment.

As day turned to night and the hours stretched on, her hope for rescue began to wane. The silence of the mountain was deafening, broken only by the sound of her labored breathing and the distant echoes of her own thoughts.

In the midst of her isolation and despair, her mind wandered to conjuring ways of getting down. She imagined the feel of solid ground beneath her feet, the essence of freedom in the wind. But as the moments ticked by, the truth of her plight loomed larger than ever, casting a darkness over her hopes and dreams.

Then, just when her resolve was on the verge of breaking, a flicker of movement caught her eye. She looked on in stunned disbelief as a helicopter appeared on the horizon, its rotors slicing through the air with a deafening roar.

Hope surged within Rachel as she waved frantically, her voice hoarse as she shouted for help. But her break was short-lived as the chopper veered off course, its trajectory leading it straight into the cliff face not far from her.

The impact was thunderous, a cacophony of metal and rock colliding in a violent explosion of sound and fury. Her pulse thrummed in her ears as she witnessed, in misery, a fiery eruption. Her breath caught in her throat as the wreckage unfolded before her eyes.

And then, as if emerging from a nightmare, more figures appeared amidst the ruins. Her blood ran cold as she realized the truth. The world was in the grip of a zombie apocalypse, and she was trapped in the heart of it.

With each passing moment, Rachel's desperation grew, her mind racing for a solution. But as the hours stretched on and rescue seemed increasingly unlikely, boredom set in, gnawing at her sanity with relentless persistence.

In a desperate bid to distract herself from the grim circumstances of her situation, her gaze fell upon a cluster of loose rocks within arm's reach. With a fleeting notion of whimsy, she reached out, her fingers curling around the rough edges of a stone.

And then, with a sudden burst of inspiration, Rachel began to juggle. The stones flew through the air in a mesmerizing dance, their movements fluid and graceful against the backdrop of the cliff face. For a moment, she felt a sense of freedom, a momentary respite from the chaos and uncertainty that surrounded her.

But as she lost herself in the rhythm of her juggling performance, disaster struck in the form of an abrupt gust of wind. With a sickening crash, one of the rocks veered off course, its trajectory altered in an instant.

Rachel's eyes widened in horror as she watched helplessly, her breath catching in her throat as the rock collided with her head with brutal force. Pain exploded behind her eyes, stars dancing across her vision as she flopped backward. Her legs and arms dangled like a droopy bird, her grip on the cliff face faltering. While she was knocked out, her mind convinced her she had made it to the top with Kiki, so she began to undo her harness. When the weight of her plummeting took hold, her eyes fluttered open to a dizzying blur of motion.

The world spun around her in a disorienting whirlwind as she fought to maintain her balance, her fingers clawing desperately at the rough surface of the cliff. But it was too late. The momentum of her fall carried her inexorably toward the void below.

In the final moments before impact, her mind raced with a jumble of emotions. She thought of Kiki, her dear friend lost to the horrors of the undead. She reflected on her own dreams and aspirations, the life she had hoped to build in the wake of their climb.

And then, with a bone-jarring collision, Rachel's reality went dark.

Zombie Movie & TV Trivia Answers: Round 12

1. Billy Connolly.
2. Wade Vogel.
3. Big Daddy.
4. *Fido.*
5. Playing baseball.
6. Dan O'Bannon.
7. Robert Neville.
8. *Warm Bodies.*
9. The virus is called The Solanum Virus.
10. Berkeley.

Chapter 25

Gloria, a woman in her mid-thirties, found herself navigating the treacherous streets of the zombie apocalypse with a peculiar challenge. Constantly sniffing, wheezing, and sneezing, she struggled to understand the cause of her symptoms amidst the chaos of the undead.

As she moved cautiously through the deserted cityscape, her senses on high alert, she couldn't shake the feeling of unease that lingered in the air. Every shadow appeared to conceal a lurking threat, and any rustle of movement sent a cold shiver through her. Despite her best efforts to remain composed, her body betrayed her with each wheeze and sniffle, serving as a reminder that unseen danger was always around the corner.

As she coughed her way through the living dead hordes, deftly dodging decomposing limbs like a seasoned boxer evading raindrops, Gloria made her way to safety. Navigating through the eerie silence of the abandoned city with heightened senses, she stumbled upon a couple of zombies. Their mere proximity triggered an immediate and intense allergic response. Her nose erupted into a torrent of sneezes and her eyes welled up with tears, swelling into inflamed red orbs. Her throat constricted with each ragged breath.

Armed with a tissue in one hand and a bronchodilator in the other, she attempted to tiptoe past the undead horde, but her attempts were unsuccessful. Her sniffing and gasping betrayed her presence at every turn, alerting the ghouls to her whereabouts and setting off a frantic cat-and-mouse chase through the desolate streets.

Gloria tried to camouflage herself among a cluster of infected by imitating their groans, but her efforts blew up in her face when she let out an uncontrollable sneeze. The deadheads went into a frenzy as she revealed her position.

She scrambled away from the advancing rotters, putting distance between them. Looking over her shoulder, she saw them searching for her. She held her hands to her face and coughed, then got going again. Her wild footsteps almost made her fall when she kicked a metal beam. Underneath it was a zombie. She regarded it with caution, seeing it had no legs. Despite its obvious handicap, the ghoul's upper body continued to writhe and thrash about, its dead eyes fixed hungrily on her as it strained against its metallic prison.

Drawing upon a reserve of courage she didn't know she possessed, she knelt, meeting the gaze of the abomination before her. The thing's mangled features contorted as it snarled like a rabid dog. In spite of the horror, she found the resilience of the mutilated monstrosity oddly fascinating. Withholding another sneeze, she let out a series of wheezes. Then she coughed, sending a splattering of spittle over the creature's face.

With a tilt of her head, she reached for some tissues she had in her pocket and offered them to the creature so it could wipe away the festering filth that dribbled from its torn lips. Her nose wrinkled in disgust at the noxious odor emanating from its decaying flesh, filtering up her nostrils. She could feel the imminent irritation.

She couldn't understand why she appeared to be allergic to the undead. Upon closer investigation, she believed it was the decomposing particles released by the zombies that were triggering her reactions, similar to the toxins emitted by mushrooms. As she considered this revelation, a sneezing attack overtook her and she recoiled inward, trying to lessen the noise she was making. However, her efforts failed when her mouth opened with a hacking cough that she couldn't stop.

In a panic, she got to her feet, her pulse racing as she searched for a place to hide. The sound of her coughs echoed through the desolate landscape, drawing the attention of other undead close by. Their guttural moans grew louder with each passing moment. With every step, she could feel the weight of their incessant pursuit pressing down on her, driving her forward with a single-minded commitment to escape the clutches of death once again.

Desperate for a way out, she spotted a bus nearby and made a run for it, expecting to find temporary refuge. As she slid underneath it, she realized she was not alone. A biter lay beside her, its decaying face inches away. In a panic, she tried to roll out from under the coach, but another ghoul blocked her path. As she struggled to free herself, she sneezed, and her snot sprayed the zombie in the face, temporarily blinding it and allowing her precious seconds to escape.

Despite the craziness of her situation, she remained determined to outsmart the deadheads, even if it meant resorting to unconventional tactics.

Gasping for breath, she spotted a crate of fireworks and seized the opportunity. With a mix of brilliance and sheer desperation, she concocted a plan to distract the ghouls by tossing lit firecrackers at them, aiming to divert their attention.

With fumbling hands, she lit the bangers and hurled them at the oncoming horde of zombies. By igniting the decomposing parts of the infected, the firecrackers created a surprising explosion of spore-filled clouds around her. The irritation coming from them led to her developing a lingering hacking cough. But the undead only became further riled, sparking and sizzling as they stumbled towards her.

In her frantic attempt to fend off the walkers with sparklers, Gloria inhaled a dense cloud of toxic zombie dust, inducing a catastrophic anaphylactic reaction. As the noxious particles infiltrated her lungs, her airways constricted, leaving her struggling for breath. Her chest tightened with each labored inhalation, while a searing pain radiated through her sinuses.

A violent sneezing fit racked her body, causing her to double over in agony as her throat swelled and her eyes watered uncontrollably. Gasping for oxygen became an impossible struggle. Gloria's vision blurred and her head swam with dizziness. She collapsed, heaving, puffing, and snorting. No air entered her swollen windpipe.

All the noise she made attracted the attention of every reanimated corpse within a mile radius. Her doom was sealed in a whirlwind of tissues and inhaler puffs.

Zombie Movie & TV Trivia: Round 13

1. In the film *Dawn of the Dead* (1978), where does the group of survivors take refuge?
2. Who directed the 2007 film *Planet Terror,* part of the *Grindhouse* double feature?
3. In the TV series *The Walking Dead,* what is the primary cause of reanimation in the zombies?
4. Who directed the movie *The Dead Don't Die*?
5. In *Resident Evil,* what is the name of the artificial intelligence that controls the Hive?
6. What is the nickname given to the gas station attendant zombie who becomes self-aware in *Land of the Dead* (2005)?
7. Which 1993 comedy-horror film features a zombie who becomes a private detective?
8. What country does the movie *28 Weeks Later* primarily take place in?
9. Who directed the 1981 film *The Evil Dead,* which combines horror with comedy and features a group of friends vacationing in a cabin?
10. Where does *Dead Snow* take place?

Answers will be found after the next tale.

Chapter 26

In the corner of the bar, a figure barely reaching the height of the counter nursed his liquor with a solemnity that seemed out of place for such a jovial setting. This was Tim, whose small frame belied a spirit as resilient as it was troubled. He downed drink after drink, each sip a vain attempt to numb the ache in his heart.

Only an hour earlier, he had auditioned for the role of Grumpy and was told he was too short for that part. The rejection stung more than the whiskey burning down his throat, leaving behind a bitter aftertaste of inadequacy.

As he sat there, lost in his thoughts, the laughter and chatter around him seemed like a cruel mockery of his solitude. The raucous merriment of the other patrons served only to deepen his sense of alienation. Yet, amidst the sea of revelry, Tim remained steadfast in his resolve to drown his sorrows in alcohol.

With each passing moment, the weight of his disappointment bore down on him like a heavy cloak. He couldn't shake off the anger from being overlooked, dismissed simply because of his stature. And so, he looked for comfort in the bottom of his glass, hoping to find temporary refuge from the harsh realities of a world that seemed determined to remind him of his perceived shortcomings.

As the night wore on, the atmosphere grew tense, the air thick with an eerie foreboding. Unbeknownst to Tim, the outside world was descending into madness. The apocalypse had begun, and the streets were overrun with the undead. To drown out the mounting sense of dread, he sought solace in his liquor, consuming more with each passing minute.

In his intoxicated stupor, he remained unaware. He staggered around the bar, narrowly avoiding the grasping hands of the zombies that had gotten in as if by the luck of a four-leaf clover. In his drunken state, Tim's mind wandered to a simpler time, a time of innocence and carefree play. In his imagination, he was transported back to preschool, where the world was a playground and every moment held the promise of adventure.

With a childlike enthusiasm, he stood on his chair, his small form barely rising above the tabletop, and he began to count to ten with exaggerated somberness. His voice echoed through the bar, a whimsical melody amidst the chaos unfolding around him.

As he reached the final number, he leaped off the seat with a gleeful shout, his movements clumsy yet filled with boundless energy. Like a mischievous sprite, he darted across the floor and scrambled underneath a nearby table, giggling uncontrollably as he crawled on all fours.

Beneath the table, he experienced a surge of exhilaration coursing through his veins. It was as if he had unlocked a hidden talent, a superpower that allowed him to evade danger with ease. As the undead lumbered by, their groans were drowned out by the raucous screams of the other customers. Tim perceived the cacophony as joyful celebration, convinced it was a boisterous bunch of men out on a stag night.

With a mischievous grin, he snuck through the maze of legs and chairs, his actions swift and nimble despite the haze of alcohol clouding his senses. The infected stumbled past, their movements sluggish and uncoordinated, no match for Tim's drunken agility.

Then, with a sudden burst of intoxicated inspiration, he clambered onto the bar, sloshing beer everywhere as he went. He whooped with delight, believing he was the star of some bizarre game. With wild abandon, he slid over the sticky surface, dodging the outstretched hands of the living dead reaching for him.

He then stood on a tabletop facing a horde of undead—but in his eyes, they were drinking and laughing. In a moment of boozy haze, Tim's gaze fell upon one zombie that was trying to reach him. He mistook the extended arms as an offering of more liquor. He bent down, snatching a half glass of whiskey, and downed it, throwing the empty tumbler across the room. He stumbled backward, his mind clouded by a fog of alcohol-induced cockiness.

In an truly over-the-top act, he unzipped his pants and unleashed a torrent of urine onto the unsuspecting undead, mistaking their decaying forms for the sterile confines of a bathroom stall. The acrid scent of ammonia filled the air, mingling with the putrid stench of decay as his stream cascaded over their rotting flesh. As his body swayed precariously on unsteady legs, Tim teetered on the brink of disaster, his balance hanging by a thread.

With a drunken laugh, he almost fell into the waiting arms of a now covered-in-piss deadhead. But in that moment of peril, Tim's laughter rang out like a defiant battle cry, an indication of his blind drunkenness. With a careless shrug, he finished his business over the rotten corpse, his urine mingling with the pooling blood of victims, which he believed was spilled drinks.

As he zipped up his pants with a nonchalant flick of his wrist, he surveyed the scene before him with a sense of detached amusement. The zombies writhed and groaned with hunger, their movements sluggish and disjointed as they struggled to catch him.

Empowered by his inebriated state, he leaped off the table and wove his way through the slow crowd of ghouls. With a mischievous grin, he slapped their backsides as he passed, eliciting a combination of groans and failed attempts from the deadheads trying to grab him. He mixed up the sounds of screaming and crying for cheering and applause that rang in his ears. To his delight, he believed he was the life of the party, the undisputed champion of his own show.

In a moment of drunken foolishness, Tim spotted a plastic chair in the corner of the bar. With a gleeful shout, he mistook it for a swing in a park and made a beeline for it. With a clumsy flourish, he threw himself onto the stool, only to become stuck. Hysterical laughter set in as he struggled to free his body, his legs tangled in the gaps between the seat. He let out an "Oomph" as he toppled over, crashing to the floor in a heap.

As he lay there in fits of chuckles, he saw the zombies closing in. At first, he perceived them as bar staff and assumed he'd be helped out of the chair. But as they got closer he finally picked up on their snarling. He knew then that what he was seeing wasn't what he had thought. He squeezed his eyes tight, reopened them with clarity, and realized the horrifying truth when an undead bit into his leg.

Zombie Movie & TV Trivia Answers: Round 13

1. A shopping mall.
2. Robert Rodriguez.
3. The reanimation is caused by an unknown virus.
4. Jim Jarmusch.
5. The Red Queen.
6. Big Daddy.
7. *My Boyfriend's Back.*
8. United Kingdom.
9. Sam Raimi.
10. In the mountains of Norway.

Chapter 27

Wendy, a handicapped but resilient woman thrust into the maelstrom of the zombie apocalypse, found herself navigating the interior of a high-rise building. She had taken the elevator to the 200th floor when the end-of-the-world plague started, leaving her stranded in her wheelchair as the power flickered and died.

With a sense of unease, she wheeled over to the fire exit, hesitating at the threshold as she contemplated the intimidating prospect of descending the stairs. As she surveyed her surroundings, she couldn't help but let out a nervous chuckle at the thought of going down them. "Well, this should be interesting," she muttered, flashing a wry grin as she pondered the logistics of the daunting task.

All at once an office door nearby crashed open and a zombie appeared through a cloud of dust and debris. Wendy was not one to go down without a fight. With a steely glint in her eye, she seized the opportunity to turn the tables on her undead assailant. With a quick pivot of her chair, she rammed into the ghoul with all the force she was able to muster, sending it crashing into the nearest wall with a satisfying thud.

As the reanimated corpse struggled to regain its footing, she didn't hesitate. With a triumphant cry, she revved up her wheelchair and charged forward, running over the rotter not once, not twice, but three times for good measure. "Take that, you rotting menace!" she cheered, a grin spreading across her face as she declared victory.

Satisfied the biter was 'double-dead', she pushed herself to the fire exit, peering again down the ominous stairwell. "Piece of cake," she whispered with forced confidence, even though her shaky hands betrayed her true feelings.

Driven by her own bravado, she wheeled closer, preparing for her daring descent. "Here goes nothing!" she exclaimed, without realizing that 'nothing' might be what awaited her at the bottom. With a deep breath, she inched the front wheels over the first step, using her arms to raise them, and then performed a bunny-hop maneuver with the back end of her wheelchair, each successive bounce carefully calculated to navigate down the steps.

When she reached the first landing, she detected a sudden commotion behind her. To her horror, another zombie was now somersaulting after her in a wild frenzy, his limbs whipping about like propellers. "Oh, come on!" she shouted. Ignoring the undead threat behind her, she flexed her arm muscles, lifting the front of the mobility aid and propelling herself forward. But this time she misjudged the space, causing the chair to tilt unexpectedly. She found herself hurtling down the stairs as if on a rollercoaster ride.

When she reached the next landing, her heart sank as she examined the damaged back wheels, which left her with a wobbly and useless means of escape. "Well, isn't this unlucky," she muttered, gazing wide-eyed heavenward in exasperation.

With no time to think, she hoisted her body out of the seat and began to slide down the stairs on her bum. Each step jarred her spine and sent shockwaves of agony through her tailbone. "At least my legs are already paralyzed," she groaned. Behind her, the zombie continued its insistent pursuit, its clumsy descent causing a deafening racket in the stairwell. "Can't a girl catch a break?" she moaned.

When she reached the bottom of another flight, her strength gave out. Gasping for breath, she took a moment to regain her vigor. She glared up at the approaching infected one with a mixture of annoyance and resignation.

In a final act of desperation, Wendy turned to face the advancing biter, its vacant eyes locked on her with hungry anticipation. "You've got to be kidding me!" she yelled, shaking her head in disbelief as the undead creature lurched toward her. Stretching up from the landing, she latched onto a door handle and pulled herself into a hallway. With every ounce of her energy, she twisted her body until she was all the way in. Then she pushed the door closed, leaning against it as she took a moment to catch her breath.

After a minute, she gazed around and realized she was in an office area that was being remodeled. The floor was littered with debris, and exposed wiring snaked along the walls like menacing serpents. Determined to escape the pursuing zombie, she began to crawl forward, her paralyzed legs dragging uselessly behind her. With each agonizing movement, she pulled herself closer to the center where construction tools were scattered about.

Her eyes scanned the dispersed equipment for anything that could aid her getaway. Amidst the chaos, she spotted a nail gun lying on the ground, its sleek design unfamiliar in her hands. Without hesitation, she picked it up, her fingers fumbling over the foreign controls. Anticipation drove her as she held the device at close range, inspecting it and trying to decipher its workings in the heat of the moment. Confusion clouded her mind as she struggled to unlock the mechanism, her panic mounting with each passing second.

Finally, with a click, the safety released, and she let out a sigh of relief. But in her haste, her finger remained firmly pressed against the trigger. In a flash of horrifying awareness, she realized her mistake too late. With a deafening roar, it fired, and a sharp pain exploded in her forehead as a nail embedded itself in her skull. She howled in agony, drawing the attention of a construction worker zombie. Its lifeless eyes fixated on the source of fresh blood. In an attempt to defend herself, she turned the gun on the advancing undead, but the feeble ammunition did little to deter its advance.

With her options dwindling and fear coursing through her veins, she grasped for anything else within reach. Her digits latched onto a spray foam insulation device lying nearby, its unfamiliar appearance piquing her curiosity. Without a second thought, she aimed the nozzle at the approaching zombie, hoping to thwart it with a blast of whatever stuff the gadget contained.

With a firm press of the trigger, a stream of thick matter shot out, enveloping the ghoul in a rapidly expanding mass. As the froth solidified, it continued to maneuver toward her, its lumbering steps cracking the hardened substance beneath its bulk. The sound, akin to snapping branches, echoed through the room and sent an icy chill down Wendy's back.

She stared in shock as the creature closed in on her, its twisted form an ugly sight and the odor of the spray filtering up her nose. A headache struck her and her eyes began to water, the chemical she'd used seeping into her lungs. She let out a series of coughs, and her chest started to feel heavy.

Without warning, the deadhead toppled over, crashing down on her with a sickening thump. The impact knocked the wind out of her, leaving her gasping for breath below the weight of the congealed mass of the zombie. Panic surged through her incapacitated body as she struggled to push the monstrosity off of her, but the substance held it firmly in place, trapping her underneath.

Despair clawed at her mind as she realized the precariousness of her situation. With the creature pinning her down, she was defenseless against the looming threat of another undead in the room. "You've got to be kidding me!" she howled again, as the sound of its approaching footsteps grew closer. The hungering moans of another zombie grew louder as it closed in on her.

As she lay trapped beneath the foam-covered zombie, she yelled, "Fantastic, what a way to go out!" Coughing and swallowing hard, she mustered her strength to add, "Fuck you, world!" before a scream ripped through her as the flesh-eater sank its teeth into her arm.

Zombie Movie & TV Trivia: Round 14

1. In *Zombieland,* what is the iconic rule #2 that Tallahassee follows?
2. Which 2014 Australian film follows a zombie apocalypse survivor seeking sanctuary in the Outback?
3. What is the occupation of the main character, Lionel, in the film *Dead Alive* (1992)?
4. In the film *Pontypool,* what unique method do the zombies use to spread the infection?
5. Who directed the 1992 film *Braindead,* known for its over-the-top gore and humor in dealing with zombies?
6. In *The Walking Dead* TV series, what is the primary mode of transportation used by the survivors?
7. What is the title of the first zombie movie ever made, released in 1932 and directed by Victor Halperin?
8. What unusual item does Lionel use to fight off zombies during the memorable lawnmower scene?
9. In *World War Z,* who plays Gerry Lane?
10. What is the primary setting for the 2016 South Korean zombie film *Train to Busan*?

Answers will be found after the next tale.

Chapter 28

In the sleepy town of Bookshire, Dave, dubbed The Library Lover, was an oddity. He cherished the scent of aged pages, the whispered tales of ancient tomes, and the faint aroma of parchment that lingered in the air of the local library. To him, the library wasn't just a building, it was a sacred haven, a sanctuary where he could escape the chaos of the outside world and immerse himself in the comforting embrace of literature.

When the apocalypse struck like a ton of zombie-infested bricks, Dave was as unprepared as a goldfish in a shark tank. The once tranquil streets transformed into battlegrounds, swarming with the undead and desperate survivors clinging to life like koalas to eucalyptus trees. But amidst the mayhem, he perceived an opportunity to turn the tide and carve out a safe haven amid the storm of rotters.

Drawing inspiration from his beloved novels, he devised a strategy to fortify the library into an impregnable fortress against the encroaching hordes of zombies. With a passion rivaling a teenager's obsession with their favorite band, he stacked literature in intricate patterns to create a complex maze that would baffle even the most determined of invaders.

Books of all shapes and sizes became masonry in his makeshift walls, their spines forming a patchwork barrier that snaked through the library like a demented game of Tetris. Secret passages and hidden chambers were woven into the fabric of his structure, providing him with escape routes and vantage points from which to survey his domain.

As days turned into weeks and the library evolved into a literal fortress of knowledge, he grew confident in his ability to outsmart the zombies. And he still had enough food, since the bank of vending machines in the break room had recently been restocked. He patrolled the tangled corridors with the swagger of a cowboy in a spaghetti western, his footsteps echoing off the walls like the beat of a war drum.

To the casual observer, it seemed as though the library itself had come to life—a living, breathing entity pulsating with the energy of defiance. He would do anything to protect the pages within. But for all his meticulous planning and tireless efforts, he overlooked one crucial detail—the element of structural weakness.

While he prowled the passageways of his citadel one night, he failed to anticipate the presence of a lone zombie lurking in the shadows. Its darkened eyes fixed on him with a greedy hunger. In that moment, Dave thrust himself at the creature and gripped tightly to the book that was in the clutches of the corpse.

He was locked in a desperate tug-of-war with a relentless rotter. He gritted his teeth and pulled with all his might, refusing to relinquish the hardback to the undead intruder.

"No!" he shouted. But the flesh eater persisted, its grip unwavering as it shuffled and tugged, the stale scent of decay filling the air.

"Not on your life," he growled through clenched jaws, his muscles straining with effort. "You can't have it. It is MINE!" The words came out as a defiant roar, punctuated by grunts of exertion.

As the struggle continued, he found himself dangerously close to the deadhead, with mere inches separating them. He could see the creature's rotten core, the skin decomposing before his eyes, and the stench made his nose wrinkle in disgust.

"If you drop it," he panted, beads of sweat trickling down his brow, "I'll let you bite me." But the revenant remained unfazed, its grip unwavering as it persisted to pull with tireless moans and groans.

With a sinking heart, he realized he couldn't win the battle of tug-of-war. With a resigned sigh, he released his grasp on the book and hastily retreated, darting behind one of his towering publication fortresses for cover.

He peered cautiously from his hiding spot. His cheeks flushed hot as he witnessed the zombie drop the novel to the ground with a careless thud. With a sickening crunch, the undead creature stomped over the volume, its decomposing foot grinding the pages beneath its weight as it searched for Dave. The sight was a painful reminder of the ineffectiveness of his efforts to protect the precious books within the library's walls.

Holding his breath, he remained hidden, his mind racing with anger and frustration. As the ghoul shuffled past, its attention diverted elsewhere, he let out a silent sigh of relief, grateful to have evaded detection for now.

An hour passed with no sign of where the walker had gone until it suddenly appeared across from him. In a moment of sheer panic, Dave lunged for the nearest weapon—a hefty tome that lay abandoned on a nearby shelf.

He swung the book with all the force he had the ability to muster, hoping to strike the revenant down before it sank its teeth into his flesh. Realizing what he had done, he almost fainted. The very items he had vowed to protect, he had launched at a decomposing skin bag.

He rushed to pick up the book and nearly got bitten. Reluctantly leaving it behind, he had to think of another way to fend off the zombie.

While he paced an aisle deep in thought, he lost his footing on a pile of bookends and stumbled headlong into the path of the oncoming corpse. With a sickening crack, he collided with the undead creature. The impact jolted him, causing stars to dance before his eyes and leaving him momentarily dazed. They both tumbled to the ground in a tangled heap.

As they struggled to disentangle themselves from one another, he sensed cold fear creeping over him—a sense of impending doom that he could no longer ignore.

He gathered as many books as he could, and when an arm grabbed him, he tried to slap it away, but it refused to let go. He knew he had to drop the pile of literature he held onto for dear life, but he couldn't bring himself to do it.

He backed up into a towering masterpiece of his own craftsmanship. The tower wobbled, swayed, and then collapsed, burying him under a collection of heavy novels. Taking deliberate care not to bend any covers or tear pages, he pushed them aside, inadvertently allowing access for the undead to reach him.

He tried to squirm away, but with a swamped sense of dread, he realized he had become ensnared in his own trap, a victim of his own hubris and the relentless march of the living dead. His fortress was no match for the biters. In fact, a rat would have disintegrated it.

While clutching a series of tales, he met his demise in the very place he had sought to protect—a casualty of his own stubbornness and the insatiable hunger of the infected horde. As his consciousness faded into oblivion, he could only hope that his legacy would live on.

Zombie Movie & TV Trivia Answers: Round 14

1. Double tap.
2. *Wyrmwood: Road of the Dead.*
3. He works in a zoo.
4. Through infected words and language.
5. Peter Jackson.
6. Horses.
7. *White Zombie.*
8. Lionel uses a modified, super-powered lawnmower to fight off zombies in the iconic lawnmower scene.
9. Brad Pitt.
10. A train.

Chapter 29

Emily, known as Lady Liberty, had captivated audiences worldwide with her unparalleled ability to slip free from the most confounding restraints. Whether it was handcuffs or straitjackets, she had earned the title of the Queen of Liberation.

Fresh from a show in Las Vegas, she had returned to Boston just as the apocalypse unfolded. Amidst the chaos of the zombie-infested city, she stumbled upon an abandoned psychiatric facility, its eerie ambiance thick with the unsettling echoes of its past. As she traversed the darkened halls, she came across a viewing room with padded walls, the remnants of a discarded straitjacket catching her eye.

With cautious steps, she entered the room and approached the restraint, her mind buzzing with ideas. Suddenly, the door creaked open and she instinctively spun around, ready to defend herself. Her tension eased at the sight of an orderly entering the room.

"What are you doing in here?" The man's voice was gruff, his eyes narrowing as he surveyed her.

"Um, nothing." Emily's response came out as a nervous stutter, her fingers tightening over the garment.

"Why are you holding that restraining jacket? Are you a patient?" His tone was accusatory, suspicion evident in his gaze.

Her mind raced as she tried to come up with a convincing explanation. "No! I ran in here to escape those undead things. I just happened to grab this," she gestured awkwardly to the restraint, her voice tinged with desperation. "Look, you might recognize me. I'm rather famous. I'm Lady Liberty, the female version of Harry Houdini."

The orderly's expression remained unchanged, his skepticism clear. "Never heard of you. I suggest you head to one of the bunkers."

"No! I'm safe here. Those deadheads can't get into this room," Emily insisted, her gaze flickering between the man and the large floor-to-ceiling viewing pane.

"It's your funeral," he remarked, before turning to leave.

"Wait, don't go, be a good fellow and help me put this on," she implored, holding up the straightjacket.

The orderly hesitated, a flicker of uncertainty crossing his features. "You must be out of your mind. That's suicide. I'm convinced you're a patient here. You have to be, to be that insane!" he exclaimed, his voice tinged with disbelief.

"I'm not crazy. I just want to have some fun. Come on, lend a hand," she pleaded. Her eyes were wide with excitement as she batted her eyelashes and flashed a girlish smile.

He remained silent for a moment, his expression unreadable. Then, with a resigned sigh, he relented. "Fine. But you have to give me a blow job. Then I'll do it," he said, his tone laced with a mixture of defiance and resignation.

Her eyes widened in shock and resentment. "Now who's the deranged one? In the middle of this apocalypse, you want to get your rocks off?" she retorted. Taking a deep breath, she walked closer to him, her voice softening. "Okay, I'll do it, but you better keep your promise."

The orderly nodded, his expression serious as he unzipped his pants. "I'm a man of honor," he said.

After she performed oral sex on him, she stood up and waited for him to help her put on the restraint. He did as promised, and when he was done, he left without uttering a word.

She shook her head in disbelief and approached the window, excitement coursing through her veins. As the first undead creature stumbled into view, she winked cheekily at it, relishing the thrill of the impending challenge. Soon, a horde of zombies gathered outside the viewing room, their decaying hands clawing at the glass in a frenzied attempt to reach her.

With a whispered giggle, Emily began her routine, expertly maneuvering to escape from the straightjacket. But her triumph was short-lived. She became ensnared on a particularly stubborn belt as she attempted to free herself. Struggling with urgent manipulations of her body, she was interrupted by the relentless pounding of the corpses colliding with the barrier. Her heart raced as the deafening thuds against the reinforced screen intensified, sending electric shocks down her legs as she realized the impending threat.

With each impact, hairline fractures snaked across the surface of the glass, resembling delicate spiderwebs beneath the unstoppable force of the undead. The once-solid frame groaned and bowed under the weight of the amassed horde, the cracks widening with every subsequent assault. Then, with a thunderous roar, the window succumbed to the overwhelming pressure, shattering into a myriad of sharp shards that crashed to the floor.

Realizing the imminent danger, Emily abandoned her attempts to untie herself and fled down the hallway, seeking refuge behind a large nurse's desk. Misery gnawed at her as she struggled to undo the buckle. Her stomach knotted, and she began to feel nauseated.

Footsteps echoed threateningly down the corridor, signaling the approaching horde. With a surge of adrenaline, she kicked out her feet in a frantic attempt to loosen the latch, unwittingly drawing the attention of the zombies to her hiding place.

Cornered and outnumbered, she sprang into action, leaping over the counter with agile grace as the flesh eaters closed in on her. Racing for the exit, she found that she was surrounded by a pack of ravenous undead, their hungry groans filling the air.

With quick thinking, she darted outside and toward an abandoned ambulance, flinging open the doors without hesitation. Inside, she discovered she was face-to-face with a reanimated patient. His outstretched arms grasped for her, but the man was belted into the bed, unable to reach her despite his desperate attempts.

Ignoring the imminent threat, she positioned herself opposite the man, using his inability to get at her to her advantage. As she struggled to free her body from the straightjacket, a daring idea sparked in her mind.

Kneeling in front of him, she offered her upper stomach in the hope that the creature would gnaw through the belt restraining her. With bated breath, she watched as the zombie chewed through the fabric, each bite bringing her closer to freedom.

With a wriggle and a pull, she freed herself from the stuck loop, her fingers fumbling in urgency to remove the restraint. Dropping it to the floor, she let out a cry of victory. Unaware that she was making a lot of noise, she drew the attention of the undead. She gazed at the open doors, facepalming her forehead for not having closed them. Two zombies suddenly appeared and she gulped in surprise, their hungry growls filling the confined space.

Panic surged through her as she fought against the relentless onslaught of the deadheads, their gnashing teeth inches away from her flesh. One of them had penetrated her skin on her ankle, but she was so hyped up with fear that she hadn't realized she had been bitten. With a final burst of strength, she pushed the creatures aside and fled into the night, her body pulsating with adrenaline.

Yet as she raced through the desolate streets, a creeping dread settled over her. With each passing moment, she could feel the insidious change taking place, her humanity slipping away as the infection coursed through her veins. Collapsing to her knees, Emily knew that her days as Lady Liberty were over.

Zombie Movie & TV Trivia: Round 15

1. In *28 Days Later,* where does Jim wake up to find London deserted?
2. Which 2004 horror-comedy film features a group of medical students trying to find a cure for reanimation?
3. What is the title of the 2018 South Korean animated film that tells the story of a zombie apocalypse from the perspective of a zombie?
4. Who played the role of Tallahassee in the film *Zombieland*?
5. What is the name of the protagonist in the video game series *Dead Rising*, known for battling hordes of zombies in various settings?
6. In *World War Z*, what is the occupation of Gerry Lane (Brad Pitt) before the outbreak?
7. Name three famous actors in the movie *The Dead Don't Die.*
8. What is the primary objective of the characters in the 2009 film *Pontypool*?
9. In *The Walking Dead* comics (the basis of the TV show), who is the leader of the Hilltop community?
10. Which 1992 film directed by Peter Jackson features a group of friends fighting off zombie hordes in their neighborhood?

Answers will be found after the next tale.

Chapter 30

Fred, a lone homebody after the death of his wife, often referred to himself as The Gardening Guru. He reveled in the vibrant splendor of his lush garden, a sanctuary where he tenderly nurtured an array of flora with unwavering devotion. The garden was his haven, filled with the intoxicating fragrance of blooming flowers and the soothing rustle of leaves that whispered secrets of growth and life.

Under the harsh glare of the midday sun, he crouched in the corner of his office, sweat dripping down his back. The neighborhood had descended into a living nightmare, overrun by hordes of ravenous zombies in search of their next meal. Their gruff groans and moans caused the hairs on Fred's arms to rise, sending a chilling sensation across his back. He huddled in the room, his muscles tensed as he thought of a way to sneak past them.

With a sense of dread gnawing at his insides, he knew he had to escape before it was too late. Every inch of his house was riddled with the dead, like an infestation of maggots. The front door stood between him and the relative safety of the outside world, but it was also the gateway to the unknown horrors that lurked beyond. Steeling himself, he had no choice but to take the risk.

With deliberate, slow, and cautious steps, he edged toward the door. The air was thick with tension, the only sound being the distant hum of flies buzzing around the decaying corpses that littered his house. With unsteady hands, he reached for the doorknob, the metal hot to the touch in the blistering heat.

With a silent prayer on his lips, he turned the knob and eased the door open, the hinges protesting with a soft squeak that seemed to echo for miles. He peered out into his front yard, his heart sinking like a stone in his chest as he realized what had happened. What had been a source of pride and joy, his prized garden, was now ruined beyond repair.

His flowerbed, once a riot of color and fragrance, was now nothing more than a tangle of broken stems and trampled petals. The delicate blooms he had nurtured with such care were crushed beneath the heavy tread of the undead, their vibrant hues muted to a sickly shade of brown.

His vegetables were strewn about like discarded rubbish, their leaves torn and shredded by the marauding zombies. Carrots lay uprooted and scattered across the ground, their bright orange flesh exposed to the harsh sunlight. Tomatoes, plump and ripe for picking, had been smashed to pulp under the weight of the ghouls' feet. He counted thirty rotters, and for a while, he wasn't sure what he would do, where he would go.

Looking beyond his property, he witnessed even more creatures ambling about like lost, dead souls.

Fred's gaze returned to his yard, his heart aching as he surveyed the devastation before him. His beautiful garden was reduced to a desolate wasteland by the flesh-eaters. Tears pricked at the corners of his eyes as he took in the scene. With immense sorrow, he decided to find a place to hide.

He gazed at his surroundings. Leaning against the garage wall was his spade. He scanned around, planning out his route. Then, with hasty but quiet steps, he made his way there and retrieved his tool.

With a held breath he darted to the back of his property, where an untended section awaited his attention. Overgrown and neglected, it seemed the perfect spot for his daring plan. He was pleased to see that none of the living dead had ventured into that area, but he knew it wouldn't be long before they did.

With swift determination, he plunged his spade into the earth, digging furiously as the soil gave way beneath his efforts. Three feet into the ground, he paused momentarily, straining his ears for any sign of approaching undead. Satisfied by the eerie silence, he wiped the sweat from his brow and resumed his excavation.

Having reached a depth of six feet, he deemed the hole sufficient. Dropping his tool, he set to work gathering his most despised adversaries—bamboo stems. With meticulous precision, he pulled one out and then cut it to the right length.

With his makeshift breathing apparatus in hand and his trusty shovel, he descended into the pit, the earth enveloping him as he burrowed deeper into the soil. Waist-deep in his subterranean refuge, he discarded the instrument, lay down, and began to cover the rest of himself with the loose dirt, using his hands to pack it tightly around his body.

Fully submerged in darkness and silence, save for the rhythmic thud of his racing heart, he inserted one end of the bamboo straw into his mouth, the other poking out through the soft ground above. With bated breath, he lay motionless, his senses heightened as he waited for the inevitable approach of the reanimated corpses.

Hours passed in tense anticipation, Fred's intuition attuned to the slightest movement. Unable to see or hear, he relied on his instincts and optimism that the creatures would soon abandon his property, allowing him to emerge unscathed and reinforce his house to better protect him against the deadheads.

His resolve wavered, doubts creeping into his mind like encroaching shadows. Through vibrations, he sensed the presence of the undead, his heart racing as he felt the ground above him tremble with the weight of the horde.

With every fiber of his being, Fred fought the urge to panic, forcing himself to remain still as the zombies drew closer. Sweat drenched his back, his muscles tense with anticipation as he waited for the inevitable.

Then, just as he had hoped for respite, the opposite occurred. The erratic movements of the living dead trampled over his makeshift breathing tube, crushing it beneath their rotting soles and cutting off his air supply.

Alarm surged through him as he realized he was suffocating, his frantic attempts to dig out of the hole thwarted by the weight of the deadheads standing on his freshly dug grave. Every time he scooped handfuls of dirt, it rained back down on him. His chances of escape grew slimmer by the second.

As Fred's fear mounted, his actions became frenzied, his hands clawing desperately at the stifling earth that enveloped him. His time was running out. His oxygen-deprived lungs screamed for air, his vision blurring as darkness threatened to consume him. The relentless pressure of the soil bore down on him, crushing his hopes of survival with merciless force.

In a final act of desperation, his shaky fingers grasped at the surface, his strength waning with each clump of dirt that cascaded down. With a mouthful of grit, his life fading, he closed his eyes, surrendering to the inevitable acceptance of death.

The sun rose on a world forever changed, its rays casting a golden hue upon the grounds that had once been Fred's sanctuary. Surrounded by the rubble and ruin, a single flower bloomed but was stood on by a hungry group of zombies.

Zombie Movie & TV Trivia Answers: Round 15

1. St. Thomas' Hospital.
2. *Re-Animator.*
3. *Seoul Station.*
4. Woody Harrelson.
5. Frank West.
6. UN Investigator.
7. Bill Murray, Adam Driver, Chloe Sevigny.
8. To understand and contain the virus's unique language trigger.
9. Maggie Greene.
10. *Braindead* (also known as *Dead Alive*).

Chapter 31

Grace's heart pounded against her ribs as she sprinted across the vast African plains, her breaths coming in ragged gasps. The scorching sun beat down upon her as she fled through the savanna, with the distant roars of lions and the calls of other creatures echoing in the air.

Her journey had started innocently enough, with Grace embarking on a photography expedition to capture the natural beauty of the wilderness. Little did she know that her adventure would soon devolve into a fight for survival against a horde of flesh-eating zombies that had inexplicably risen in this remote corner of the continent.

The memory of her encounter with the undead guide group made her shudder involuntarily. They had been her only connection to civilization in this unforgiving bush, but now they were nothing more than mindless predators, their vacant eyes fixed on her with an insatiable hunger.

For days, she managed to evade the relentless chase of the living dead, relying on her survival instincts to navigate the treacherous terrain. Eventually, starvation and thirst drove her toward a nearby watering hole. With extreme caution, she approached and paused to catch her breath, scanning the area for any signs of danger. The surface of the pond shimmered in the scorching sunlight.

Using her hands, she cupped water in her palms, gulping down the cool liquid as relief flooded through her parched body. For a fleeting moment, she allowed herself to believe that she might have found sanctuary in this secluded corner of the African plains. She sat at the edge of the water contemplating her next move. Then the unmistakable sound of the undead closed in, prompting her to take off running.

While she navigated the savanna, her senses were captivated by a majestic sight—a herd of elephants moving in the direction of the watering hole she had just raced away from. Their massive forms cast imposing silhouettes against the backdrop of the golden sunset, their gentle trumpeting resonating through the air.

Excitement coursed through Grace as she reached for her camera, eager to capture this awe-inspiring moment. But then annoyance washed over her as she realized her Canon was nowhere to be found. She realized that she must have dropped it during her hurried escape from the zombies.

Disappointment clouded her features before she steeled herself and continued her journey through the unforgiving wilderness, her footsteps heavy with the weight of missed opportunities and lost memories.

Her eyes scanned the area for any signs of safety. In the distance, she spotted a narrow footbridge spanning a river, its weathered planks and rusted metal supports standing out against the backdrop of the landscape. Excitement coursed through her veins as she thought it a potential escape route from the pursuit of the zombie horde.

Hurrying toward the overpass, her steps quickened with hope. But when she drew closer, her heart sank to the pit of her stomach at the sight of a large warning sign looming ahead. It read in bold, threatening capital letters, 'DANGER. UNSTABLE BRIDGE. DO NOT CROSS'. She gazed to the right and left, discerning a clear path through the jungle. Lacking confidence in her ability to navigate through the foliage, she believed she would be safer taking the walkway.

But despite the visible signs of wear and tear on the weathered bridge, she chose to ignore the evidence her own eyes provided. Reassuring herself that it was merely a deterrent for tourists, or a sign planted by the locals to dissuade trespassers, she dismissed the reality of the decaying structure. With the zombies closing in behind her, she moved onto the wooden steps, positive that it would grant her a better getaway from the biters.

Each footfall on the creaking planks felt like a gamble, the air heavy with anticipation, and the sounds of her surroundings were magnified in her ears. She could hear the faint rustling of leaves in the breeze, the distant calls of birds in the canopy above, and the foreboding grating of the bridge swaying in the wind.

The wood groaned under her weight, protesting the strain of her passage. Every step forward appeared shaky, as the old timbers squeaked and shifted beneath her feet. Near the midpoint of the bridge, a sickening crack suddenly split the air, followed by the unmistakable sound of splintering boards. Horror washed over her as she realized that her foot had punched through one of the rotted planks, leaving her ankle hanging over the edge. Frozen in fear, she clutched the railing for support. Feeling the roughness of the worn rope, her breath caught in her throat as she stared down into the shadowy depths below.

As she made her way across, the warning signs become more apparent. The ropes holding the structure together showed evidence of serious wear and tear, with their frayed ends dangling ominously in the wind. Panic bubbled in her chest as she realized the imminent danger she faced. She looked down and wished she hadn't. A sense of falling washed over her, and she closed her eyes and waited for the sensation to pass.

Despite her growing unease, she pressed on, her eagerness to escape overriding her fear of heights. With each stride, the sounds of the pursuing zombies grew louder, their throaty moans echoing through the savanna. The bridge seemed to stretch on forever, every plank an uncertain foothold in her race against time.

As she advanced across, the deteriorated state of the timber became more and more noticeable. Her movements sent tremors of instability through the aged planks, causing them to protest with loud splitting and popping noises that reached her ears with menace. She sensed the wood disintegrating beneath her feet, dispatching splinters and fragments that cascaded into the depths below.

And then, in a heartbeat, disaster struck. With a deafening crack, the ropes holding the bridge aloft gave way, sending her plummeting downward into the gorge. As she splashed head-first into the river below, her stomach clenched in terror at the sight of the murky waters teeming with crocodiles, their jaws snapping in anticipation of their next meal.

In that harrowing moment, Grace's destiny was sealed. As she was dragged under the water's surface, her final view was a grim scene unfolding before her eyes. The undead, drawn by the commotion, began plummeting after her into the churning depths one by one. The water became a swirling vortex of disorder, with the crocs eagerly closing in on their unsuspecting prey.

Zombie Movie & TV Trivia: Round 16

1. What is the name of the virus that turns animals into zombies in the film *The Girl with All the Gifts*?
2. In the film *Maggie* (2015), what is the name of Arnold Schwarzenegger's character?
3. Which 1988 film, directed by Dan O'Bannon, features a zombie horde infiltrating a cemetery after a government experiment goes awry?
4. What new character joins the main group in *Zombieland: Double Tap*?
5. What is the primary reason for the zombie outbreak in the film *The Crazies* (2010)?
6. In *Resident Evil*, what is the name of the pharmaceutical company responsible for the zombie outbreak?
7. Who directed the 2016 film *The Girl with All the Gifts*?
8. What movie has Nazi zombies in snow?
9. In *Dead Set*, a British TV series about a zombie apocalypse, where do the contestants of a reality show find refuge?
10. Which famous director helmed the 1990 remake of *Night of the Living Dead*?

Answers will be found after the next tale.

Chapter 32

Harold, a 64-year-old accountant with a noticeable limp due to his age, ran with all his might through the desolate streets, his breaths ragged and labored. The fast-moving zombies pursued him with great hunger, their deep groans ringing out in the eerie silence of the apocalypse. Harold's aging body struggled to keep up with the tireless pace, his limbs protesting with each stride.

His back ached as he ducked into the entrance of an underground car park, the musty scent of decay and oppressive darkness closing in around him. The sound of his own rapid gasps bounced back off the concrete walls as he moved stealthily between abandoned vehicles, his senses heightened to the slightest noise.

Every creak of metal and shuffle of debris made his hair stand on end. His knee throbbed, and his feet hurt. He had to keep going as he navigated the tangled maze of cars, daring not to use a flashlight for fear it would draw the attention of the lurking undead. Instead, he relied solely on his hearing, straining to detect any sign of movement in the darkness.

Suddenly, a boisterous growl broke through the quietness, freezing him in his tracks. His heart slowed to a thunderous, slow-moving beat as he pressed himself against the side of a rusted van, his breath catching in his throat. The flesh eaters were close. Their ravenous hunger drove him deeper into the shadows of the underground car park.

The noisy grunts of the approaching zombies grew louder as his stomach dropped, and he burst into a frantic run. He cast a terrified glance over his shoulder, his eyes widening in horror as he saw the horde rushing toward him like an unstoppable mudslide, their twisted forms with outstretched limbs reaching for him.

With every ounce of strength he could summon, he dodged behind a large black limousine, using it as cover to catch his breath. His chest heaved as he pressed his back against the sleek metal. But his respite was cut short when a pair of zombies appeared at either side of him. Their decaying faces warped into hideous snarls as they lunged for him with extended arms.

With a surge of energy, he bolted once more, his legs pumping furiously as he raced through the maze of abandoned vehicles, his muscles burning and his knee threatening to give out.

The chase seemed endless. Every corner he turned revealed more creatures closing in on him from all sides. Taking refuge behind a fire truck, he waited with bated breath until the coast was clear before cautiously venturing to another floor of the car park. The darkness enveloped him like a suffocating cloak, the absence of light amplifying his sense of dread.

Each step felt like a leap into the unknown. His nerves stretched to their breaking point as he struggled to remain unseen and unheard by the ever-present threat of the undead.

After two hours, he managed to emerge from the underground parking. The brightness of the day gave him new hope. He could see better and believed that would help him evade the rotters. He ventured out onto the barren promenades in his search for refuge.

Several minutes had slipped by when he stumbled upon the crumbling remains of a supermarket. Harold's eyes widened with anticipation. Perhaps he might find something to quench his thirst and sustain him for a little longer during the mayhem. With caution, he limped inside.

The shelves had been looted, leaving behind only a few scattered items. Hunger clawed at his stomach as he scanned the aisles, searching for anything that could provide relief. He pivoted when the sound of rushed footsteps hit his ears, his eyes fixed on the rotters heading his way. He looked at the shelving in front of him, and his eyes fell upon a display of fly spray cans.

Without pausing to question the wisdom of his decision, he grabbed several aerosol containers and began spraying them in the direction of the approaching living dead. With a can in each hand, he didn't let go of the nozzles, the atomizers hissing as thick clouds of white mist enveloped the deadheads.

For a brief moment, the ghouls seemed to hesitate, their movements slowed by the dense fog of chemicals. His heart raced with a glimmer of hope as he proceeded to empty can after can onto the advancing horde. He struggled to catch his breath amidst the concentrated vapor, his nostrils burning with the acrid scent of the spray.

Every inhale saturated Harold's lungs with toxic fumes, sending waves of dizziness washing over him. With his eyes misted over, Harold witnessed parts of the decomposing zombies dropping in revolting clumps to the floor. The fly repellent appeared to be melting away the flesh already hanging from them.

With shock, he continued to view the fleshy, pus-filled skin as it littered the ground while they made feeble lunges through the haze. Their movements were sluggish and uncoordinated, but his own breathing grew labored, each inhale an agonizing struggle against the poison invading his respiratory system.

But the temporary reprieve was fleeting. The swarm, driven by an insatiable hunger, pushed through the cloud of insecticide with redoubled dedication. Fear clawed at his chest as he realized the ineffectiveness of his efforts.

Gasping for air, Harold stumbled through the supermarket in search of something to drink, his lungs burning from the toxic fumes. His eyes watered, and his throat constricted with painful breaths. The world spun around him as he fought to stay upright, his vision blurred with tears.

With a final desperate lunge, he fell to his knees, his body wracked with coughs as the toxins infiltrated his airways. The maddening groans of the zombies grew louder as they drew closer.

In his terminal moments, Harold cursed his own foolishness as the undead closed in, their rancid scent hot against his skin. The cans of fly spray lay scattered beside him, a cruel reminder of his weapon choice.

Harold's life flashed before his eyes as he succumbed to the overwhelming darkness. The last sound he registered was the gut-wrenching moans of the reanimated corpses.

Zombie Movie & TV Trivia Answers: Round 16

1. Ophiocordyceps.
2. Wade Vogel.
3. *The Return of the Living Dead.*
4. Madison.
5. Water contamination.
6. Umbrella Corporation.
7. Colm McCarthy.
8. *Dead Snow.*
9. The Big Brother house.
10. Tom Savini.

Chapter 33

Isabella had always been the ringmaster of her own circus, commanding attention with a flick of her wrist and a booming voice that echoed through the tent. But as the virus broke out and chaos descended upon the world outside, the fairgrounds became a haunting landscape of deserted tents and abandoned rides.

Infected clowns stumbled through the empty arena, their grotesque faces contorted into permanent grins. She ducked, dodged, and squirmed out of their grasp with an urgent agility that she never knew she possessed. She managed to get behind a bandstand, ensuring she remained hidden as she peered out.

Her nostrils stung as she inhaled, watching the surreal scene unfolding before her. A large, colorful inflatable ball, once a prop for the circus's comedic routines, now bounced erratically across the deserted midway. But instead of laughter and applause, it was now met with a chorus of grating moans and gnashing teeth as the flesh-eaters stumbled and tumbled in their dogged chase after anything living.

Despite the absurdity of the sight, Isabella couldn't bring herself to laugh. The zombies' persistence in chasing down their prey, even in the face of such comical obstacles, only served to underscore the grim realism of their greedy hunger. With a heavy heart, she turned away from the spectacle, knowing that her own survival depended on staying one step ahead of the unrelenting horde.

Moving away with caution, she got behind a tubular steel frame in red with a round wooden top, hand-painted with a star motif, and climbed atop it. Her gaze locked onto one unfortunate jester as it was bitten and transformed before her eyes. With each clumsy attempt to walk, its oversized shoes became a hindrance, causing it to trip several times. Once upon a time, that falling routine would elicit fits of laughter from the audience, but now it turned her stomach inside out. She fixed her sight on it, and she witnessed it slip on an enormous banana peel and fall into a crowd of the undead.

It was evident to her that these zombies were unlike any she'd seen in movies or read about in books. They were fast, able to climb and open doors, and they scared her more than she wanted to believe possible. Their need to annihilate, driven by their unquenchable hunger, pushed the clown aside with disjointed motions. Their rotting limbs flailed in all directions as they clamored over one another. It looked to her like they were trying to build a pyramid to get at her. Each time they reached a new height, they would tumble and try again. This left her even more unsure of what to do and where to go.

With nowhere else to turn, she abandoned her perch and ducked behind a stack of crates, her head pounding as she weighed her options. Through the gaps in the boxes, she watched as the pack descended upon an acrobatic duo, tearing into their flesh with frenzied abandon. The sound of their gruesome feast filled the air, a sickening sound of crunching bones and splattering blood.

While the creatures were busy feasting on the unfortunate pair, she thought she had a chance to slip past unnoticed, by making her escape through the front entrance while the zombies were preoccupied. But as she crouched in the shadows, her gaze focused on the central tower, its silhouette casting a long shadow across the circus tent.

The tightrope, usually reserved for skilled acrobats and daredevils, taunted her from above the expanse of the marquee as it swayed gently in the breeze. Despite never having walked a high wire in her life, Isabella felt a surge of misplaced confidence wash over her. After all, she had spent years instructing performers, guiding them through daring stunts and death-defying feats. Surely, she reasoned, she could do the same.

Ignoring the safer option of slipping past the distracted zombies and fleeing through the front entrance, she abandoned all reason and made a dash for the ladder leading up to the central tower. The undead, lost in their bloodlust, paid her no mind as she climbed higher and higher, her heart thudding in her ears with each step.

Perched atop the column, she surveyed the scene below with a mixture of dread and tenacity. The once-vibrant circus tent now lay in shambles, resembling a graveyard of memories and broken dreams. The tightrope stretched out before her, a slender thread of hope in a topsy-turvy world.

But as she took her first tentative steps onto the thin wire, her confidence began to waver. The rope swayed underneath her weight, threatening to send her tumbling to the ground. With each faltering step, she felt the eyes of the undead upon her, their hungry growls mingling with the sound of her racing heartbeat.

Panic clawed at Isabella's throat as she reached the halfway point, her trembling legs on the verge of giving way. She glanced back towards the ladder, hoping against hope for some means of escape, but the zombies had already begun their ascent, their rotting hands clawing at the metal rungs with a relentless grit.

With no other options left, Isabella pressed on, her thoughts racing with ideas of survival and self-preservation. She focused all her energy on the distant platform, willing her shaking limbs to carry her to safety. But just as she reached out for the security of solid ground, her foot slipped on the slick wire, sending her plummeting towards the waiting horde below.

In the final moments before impact, Isabella's mind flashed with memories of a life once lived, a time filled with laughter and applause. But as she fell into the outstretched arms of the undead, those recollections faded into gloom, swallowed whole by the insatiable hunger of the walking dead.

And so, in the heart of the circus tent, Isabella met her demise. Her story, like so many others, would soon be forgotten amidst the bedlam and carnage of a world overrun by the reanimated corpses.

Zombie Music Trivia: Round 1

1. Which Michael Jackson song features a zombie-themed music video?
2. What is the name of the British rock band known for their song "Zombie"?
3. In which year was the song "Zombie" by The Cranberries released?
4. Who wrote the song "Zombie"?
5. What genre is Rob Zombie known for?
6. Which Rob Zombie song features the lyrics "More human than human"?
7. What is the name of the American punk band known for their song "Zombie Nation"?
8. Which Metallica song has a reference to zombies in its lyrics?

Answers on next page.

1. "Thriller"
2. The Cranberries
3. 1994
4. Dolores O'Riordan
5. Industrial metal, heavy metal.
6. "More Human than Human"
7. G.B.H. (Charged GBH)
8. "Creeping Death"

Chapter 34

Frank, a 46-year-old pilot, had spent his life dedicated to aviation. He loved nothing more than sharing stories of his adventures in the sky with his wife and two sons. They would often gather around the dining table, laughing and chatting about his latest flights while enjoying a home-cooked meal.

On this particular evening, as he regaled his family with tales of his most recent flight, a creature smashed through the kitchen window with a bone-chilling shriek. His heart froze in his chest as he witnessed the undead lunge at his life partner, sinking its teeth into her arm with a sickening crunch.

He was knocked to the floor, his mind reeling with shock and disbelief. With no choice but to stare helplessly, he watched as his wife's eyes glazed over, her once-loving gaze now replaced by a fundamental hunger for flesh. In a haze of terror, Frank's boys entered the room, drawn by the commotion.

With a sense of dread washing over him, he was left paralyzed with fear as his wife turned to his sons, one by one, and bit into their tender limbs. The agonizing screams of his children echoed through the house, tearing at his soul as he struggled to comprehend the nightmare unfolding before him.

Driven by a primal instinct for survival, he was aware that he had no choice but to defend himself against the monstrous deadheads that had once been his clan. Still in a state of astonishment, he grabbed whatever weapons he could find, using furniture to keep the ravenous creatures at bay as he made his way to the relative safety of the bathroom.

Huddled in the darkness of the restroom, he waited in silence, his heart palpitating in his chest as he listened for any sign of movement in the rest of the house. When the sounds of chaos subsided, he cautiously emerged from his hiding place, his head numb with grief.

With sweaty hands, he sneaked downstairs, his eyes scanning the wreckage of his upturned home. Ignoring the gnawing fear in the pit of his stomach, he grabbed his car keys and headed to the garage, his only thought being to escape the terror that had consumed his family.

He climbed into his vehicle and sped off into the night, his mind obsessed with a single thought—to live. With the groans of the undead booming, he drove through the chaotic streets, his eyes fixed on the distant glow of the airfield.

He knew that his only chance of escaping the horrors that lurked in the darkness lay in reaching the safety of the airport and finding a way to evade this living nightmare. And so, with the echoes of his family's anguished cries still ringing in his ears, he pushed onward, making it to the airstrip.

He brought his car to a screeching halt and rushed into the hangar to escape the horde of undead, only to find more of them inside. With a sense of urgency that left no room for hesitation, he headed for his aircraft and threw open the door. He pulled it shut again just as a zombie tried to grab him, then sat in the cockpit. The creatures stood motionless beside his craft, their eerie moans, groans, and thumping against the metal adding to the tension.

Frank quickly went through the pre-flight checks. His usual iron-cast stomach lurched as he revs up the engines and prepared for takeoff. The airplane accelerated forward, the roar of the turbines drowning out the haunting whispers of the zombies that seemed to linger within his ears.

With a sense of relief flooding through him, he pulled back on the throttle and the plane hurtled down the runway, lifting off into the sky with a burst of speed that sent his heart racing. For a brief moment, he allowed himself to believe that he had escaped the clutches of the reanimated corpses.

Frank peered out the window, his pulse quickening. Below, the swarm moved like a writhing mass of shadows, their vacant eyes glinting in the dim light. The sight sent a chill down Frank's spine as he realized just how alone he truly was. Mourning his family gave him the strength to push through.

But as he climbed higher, the plane started to splutter and pull in jerky movements. An anchor sat in the pit of his gut as his gaze fixed on the fuel gauge. He understood with a sickening sense of dread that he had forgotten to refuel the aircraft before takeoff.

Panic gripped him as he watched the needle drop lower and lower, the engines sputtering and coughing as they struggled to keep the airplane aloft. His mind raced with fear and urgency as he came to the horrifying realization that he was running out of time.

With no other alternative, Frank became aware that he must jump at 15,000 feet and have faith that his chute would open on time, saving him from certain death. Summoning every ounce of courage he possessed, he unbuckled his seatbelt and took hold of a prepacked bag. He put it on and made his way to the door.

When he opened it, the wind rushed into his face. With a final, heart-stopping moment of hesitation, he took the plunge, hurtling toward the ground below.

He descended fast, the landscape rushing up to meet him like a hungry beast. With his parachute still untouched, Frank clung to hope, praying fervently that he might somehow steer himself to safety without deploying it too soon. But reality hit him harder than gravity ever could, and he was forced to yank the cord. The sound of the material unfurling echoed like a death knell in the stillness.

He veered hard left, but the gusts dragged him into the path of the trees. Instead of gracefully floating to the surface, he became entangled in a tree, leaving him dangling like a puppet on a string. Desperate to break out of his branch prison, he wriggled and pulled, his actions frantic as he fought to escape.

With a final, reckless swing, he managed to dislodge himself from the tangled mess, crashing to the ground with a bone-jarring thud. As if breaking both his legs wasn't enough, the parachute now resembled a sad, deflated balloon, its knotted material ensnaring two unsuspecting zombies.

As the rotters wrestled to free themselves, they dragged Frank across the uneven terrain like a hapless crash-test dummy. Trapped, injured, and surrounded by a hungry horde, he understood his time was up. With resignation settling over him like a heavy shroud, he closed his eyes, ready to face whatever awaited him in the cold embrace of the undead.

Zombie Poems: 1

Zombies groan, so does my stomach's sound,
Forget canned beans, let's strut around.
No stealth for me, just a neon parade,
"Hey zombies, come get me!" my foolish charade.

***

Tap dancing through a zombie-filled street,
Loud shoes on my feet, a heartbeat retreat.
No sneaky tiptoe, just jingles and bells,
"Hello, undead friends!" my noisy farewells.

***

Disco lights in my shelter, a zombie disco ball,
Forget barricades, we'll party 'til we fall.
No darkness for me, just a neon glow,
"Come on, zombies, let's dance!" my futile show.

***

Rollercoaster escapes, a thrill in the night,
Forget safe routes, let's go for a fright.
No planning for me, just loops and steep falls,
"Whee! Zombies, catch me!" my ride calls.

Chapter 35

Jessica and Jacob were celebrating their fifth anniversary aboard a luxurious cruise ship. They shared an insatiable passion for adventure, especially in the form of climbing. With half of the vessel now sealed off due to a rampant zombie outbreak, panic had spread among the other passengers. However, for the adventurous duo, the situation had the opposite effect. They remained unfazed by the unfolding apocalypse, ignoring repeated warnings from the ship's crew about the perilous nature of their actions. Instead, they continued to defy the rules, actively seeking out opportunities to satisfy their craving for adrenaline-fueled escapades.

On the third day, in the cool of the afternoon, with purpose in their eyes they approached the edge of the massive vessel. The salty breeze tingled their skin as they prepared for their daring stunt, to leap from one lifeboat to the next. Lowering themselves over the railing, they felt the exhilaration building as they dangled above the churning ocean below. The scent of salt mingled with anticipation, heightening their senses for the adventure ahead.

In perfect harmony, they took flight, feeling the exhilarating melody of wind and waves surround them. When they landed on the first boat, they were greeted by the dazzling show of the sun-kissed waters, its vast expanse stretching out before them like an endless canvas. With each jump across the lifeboats, they savored the sensation of enthusiasm, fueled by the adrenaline coursing through their veins.

As they glided over the boats with grace and precision, they encountered a euphoria unlike anything they had ever experienced. In that fleeting moment suspended between sea and sky, they embraced the thrill of the unknown as they indulged in the freedom of flight and the exhilarating rush of defying gravity. When they finally landed back on the deck of the cruise ship, their hearts raced and their enthusiasm soared. They were aware that they had just embarked on an adventure that would be etched in their memories forever.

The following sunny morning, their adventurous spirits led them to concoct a daring plan. Jacob would attach himself to the zipline, with Jessica holding onto him as they flew across the deck. It was clear to them that they wouldn't be allowed to attempt such a stunt, so they devised a strategy to execute it without getting caught.

Together, they approached the flying fox platform. Jess held back as the operator secured Jacob with the harness, anticipation building for the exhilarating descent. Just as Jacob prepared to plunge off the edge, Jess sprinted to him with a roguish grin and leaped onto his back.

The added momentum caused the line to sag under their combined weight, yet it held firm. With fits of giggles erupting, they were propelled across to the other side.

As soon as they landed safely, a ship's officer approached them. But they bolted, giggling like mischievous teenagers as they darted to every level, celebrating in their adrenaline-junkie excursion.

The following day, dark clouds began to form overhead and a chill crept into the air. Jessica and Jacob spotted two zombies who had breached the barricade and were ambling about on the pool deck. They observed several crew members reinforcing the barricade, while two others went after the rogue ghouls. The ominous weather did little to dampen the duo's spirits. Motivated by their daring nature, they detected an opportunity for another exhilarating jaunt.

Together, they hatched a plan to lure the undead to the tallest part of the ship with the intention of tricking them into falling overboard. As they approached the mast, an unspoken understanding passed between them. They chose to overlook the rotters for now and eagerly seized the opportunity to satisfy their climbing addiction.

While they ascended the post with Jacob taking the lead, a sudden storm descended upon them, thunder roaring in the distance and enhancing the thrill of their ascent. As rain slicked the pole, turning it into a treacherous obstacle, they exchanged a knowing glance. Undeterred, they slid down together, laughter mingling with the rush of exhilaration that coursed through their veins.

At the bottom, with their clothes drenched and their hearts pounding, they spotted the rope attached to the flagpole. Without hesitation, they grabbed it and fashioned it into a makeshift leash, binding one of the zombies that roamed the deck. With a shared grin, they began their absurd adventure, leading the snarling creature on a leash like a rabid dog.

Ignoring the confusion surrounding them as other passengers succumbed to the virus, they treated the zombie as their own bizarre pet. "Good boy," Jessica cooed, her voice a strange mixture of merriment and astonishment as they paraded the rotter around the ship. "Look at that," Jacob said, pointing out various sights to their undead companion as if it were a curious child.

They led the deadhead through the shops on the 10th floor, its growls drowned out by the din of the bustling promenade. The scent of freshly baked pastries wafted through the air from a quaint bakery, mingling with the aroma of exotic perfumes emanating from a nearby boutique. They paused to admire the gleaming displays of jewelry and designer clothing, their chuckles echoing off the polished marble floors.

From that level, they descended to the 8th where the casino beckoned with its flashing lights and cacophony of sounds. Jessica eagerly approached the roulette table, tossing chips in all directions like flying discs. She urged her pet zombie to 'fetch' with a mischievous twinkle in her eye. Jacob joined in the game, his laughter blending with the clatter of gaming tokens and the spinning of the wheel.

After turning the empty casino into their playground, they were eager for more adventures. With the living dead in tow, they made their way to another area of the ship, where they were all of a sudden faced with a horde of turned passengers.

The air was thick with the stench of decay as the reanimated mob closed in, their guttural moans sending shivers down Jacob and Jessica's spines. In a desperate attempt to control the situation, they attempted to lasso the zombies as a group, their laughter turning to panicked cries as the creatures surged forward with ravenous hunger.

But the duo's bravado proved to be their downfall. In the chaos that ensued, they were bitten as they tried to wrangle the undead horde. Blood ran down their arms and legs, while the stench of rot filled their nostrils. In that moment, they realized the blunder of their actions, but it was too late. The rush of adrenaline had led them down a path of madness from which there was no escape.

Zombie Music Trivia: Round 2

1. What is the name of the Canadian horror punk band known for their song "Zombies Ate My Neighbors"?
2. Which Iron Maiden song features a reference to zombies in its lyrics?
3. What is the name of the American metal band known for their song "Zombie Autopilot"?
4. Who released the song "I Walked with a Zombie" in 1982?
5. What is the name of the Irish rock band known for their song "Zombie"?
6. Which Megadeth album features the song "Dawn Patrol" with zombie-themed lyrics?
7. Who released the song "Zombie Ritual" in 1987?
8. What is the name of the American horror punk band known for their song "Zombie Dance"?

Answers on next page.

1. The Creepshow
2. "Still Life"
3. Unearth
4. Roky Erickson
5. The Cranberries
6. "Rust in Peace"
7. Death
8. The Cramps

Chapter 36

Fifty-eight-year-old Mike was a man of principles, a stickler for rules, and a self-appointed enforcer of order in his neighborhood. He strutted down the streets like a peacock, inspecting lawns and recycling bins with the diligence of a hawk eyeing its prey. His insistence on maintaining the pristine condition of the surroundings earned him both admiration and animosity from his neighbors. They often found themselves on the receiving end of his meticulous inspections.

With the zombie apocalypse in full force, others had fled for safety. But Mike stood his ground, determined to guard the deserted homes of his community. Armed with nothing but cans of soup and bottles of water, he embarked on his weekly food delivery rounds, a lone ranger in a world overrun by the undead.

One afternoon, as he made his circuits dropping off supplies, he glanced over at the unkempt gardens around him and sighed in exasperation at the thought of the impending yard work.

Returning home, he settled into his routine, his mind buzzing with the satisfaction of a well-executed plan. As he stepped onto his patio, the evening sun cast a warm glow over the neighborhood, a serene backdrop to soak up a day's worth of labor. As he took a seat in his oversized rocking chair, his glance swept over the street with the vigilance of a sentinel guarding his domain.

But just as he began to relax into the familiar rhythm of his customary ritual, disaster struck in the form of a sudden explosion. The eruption sent shockwaves rippling through the air, shattering the tranquility of the suburban landscape and hurling Mike from his chair with a force that left him dazed and disoriented.

As he struggled to regain his bearings amidst the pandemonium, his eyes fell upon the source of the blast—a gas pipe. With wide eyes, he watched in horror as his house went up in smoke. Without a moment's hesitation, he dashed to the back of the property to grab the yard hose, his only hope of extinguishing the inferno.

He battled the fire with the fervor of a knight defending his castle, but the gentle stream of water from the hose did little to quell the roaring blaze. In a desperate fight against the flames and the rebellious garden hose that appeared to be deliberately obstructing his actions, Mike muttered curses under his breath while he wrestled with the unruly device.

Even as he grappled with the hose, he refused to let it distract him from his mission. With a steely persistence, he continued to direct the flow of water at the advancing firestorm, each burst a testament to his unwavering resolve in the face of adversity. Choking on the clouds of smoke, he persisted.

All of a sudden, a pair of flaming zombies emerged from the conflagration, their grotesque forms illuminated by the flickering embers. With a guttural roar, they lunged towards him, their charred flesh crackling and sizzling with every step. The less-than-powerful blasts of water did little to push them back. When he backed away from them, he became entangled in the very hose he had wielded with such confidence just moments before.

With each thrash and twist, the hose wound tighter around his limbs like a boa constrictor squeezing the life out of its prey. Mike cursed his luck as he struggled with the relentless coils, his movements hampered by the weight of the hose bearing down on him.

But even as he fought against the hose's vise-like grip, he refused to yield to despair. Realizing the futility of his actions, his focus shifted to what truly mattered to him, his home. The flames continued to rage unabated, devouring everything in their path with an insatiable hunger. His thoughts were consumed by one thing, the precious supplies and important notes turning to ash within his house.

While he tussled with the hose, its coils constricting around him in a python-like hold, his behavior became more frantic and unpredictable. With each twist and turn, he felt it tightening over his body, turning him into a human pretzel. Mike toppled headfirst into the lap of the fallen zombie—a less-than-ideal landing spot.

He battled to break free from the clutches of the undead, the hose squeezing his ankles and upper legs. With every futile attempt to untangle himself, he only succeeded in becoming more entangled, his movements resembling a clumsy dance as he squirmed and writhed against the relentless coils of the hose.

And then, just when it seemed that things couldn't get any worse, the infected ones took advantage of his entrapment. With a guttural moan, one of the zombies lunged forward and sank its teeth into Mike's exposed neck. As darkness crept in at the edges of his vision, he realized with a sinking heart that this was the end.

Angered by his recklessness in fighting a house fire and the undead creatures with a garden hose, his final thoughts were of regret.

Zombie Poems: 2

A petting zoo of zombies, a cuddly affair,
Forget caution, let's show them we care.
No fear in my heart, just hugs and delight,
"Fluffy zombies, sit!" my perilous sight.

***

Who needs a map in this undead mess?
Forget directions, I'll trust GPS less.
No sense of direction, just wander and roam,
"Lost with zombies, I've found my new home."

***

Inflatable zombies to decorate my space,
Forget real threats, let's lighten the pace.
No fear in my heart, just bounce and play,
"Pop goes the undead!" my risky display.

***

Tuba tunes in the face of despair,
Forget silence, let's blare through the air.
No stealth for me, just a brass serenade,
"Zombies, enjoy the music!" my foolish crusade.

Chapter 37

Yara sat on the edge of the platform, her legs dangling over the side as she waited for her turn to bungee jump. The landscape spread out before her in a breathtaking panorama of mountains and valleys, the rugged terrain stretching as far as the eye could see. A thick canopy of vegetation blanketed the slopes, casting dappled shadows on the ground below. In the distance, she was able to catch sight of the elevator rising slowly to the summit, its cables creaking with each movement.

Beside her stood Kane, the bungy jumping operator, adjusting her harness with practiced ease. "You're all set, Yara," he said with a reassuring smile. "You can take the leap whenever you're ready."

Just as she was about to nod and make her move towards the edge, the lift doors slid open with a metallic clang. A lone figure stumbled out, its movements jerky and uncoordinated. Yara's heart skipped a beat as she recognized the telltale signs of a zombie.

The undead creature went for Kane, its vacant eyes fixed on him with a hungry intensity. Before she could react, the deadhead lunged forward, sinking its teeth into his arm with a sickening crunch. He let out a cry of pain as he slipped backward, his face contorted in agony.

She watched in horror as Kane's skin began to pale, his features contorting as the infection took hold. Within moments, he transformed into one of the living dead, his eyes glazed over, and his movements became jerky and erratic.

With a guttural growl, he lurched toward Yara, his fingers curling into claws as he tried to grab her. With a shriek of terror, she leaped over the edge and free-fell, her bungee cord stretching to its limits. The exhilaration of the fall was shortened as she witnessed reanimated corpses gathering directly beneath her suspended form.

The assembled horde gazed in confusion as she flew above them, tempting them with her aerial presence. Despite being grabbed by one of the rotters as she swung low, she managed to spring up with it still clutching her legs. She aimed a kick at it, but she still felt the piercing sensation of its fingernails gripping onto her tightly. The elastic line flung her up and down, and yet the rotter held on. As the elastic came to its end, the landing wasn't a gentle one.

The weight of Yara's realization came crashing down on her. It was a rapid descent with too much load for her cord to handle. She looked up to see the cord unraveling. The snap followed and she went plummeting to the ground with the zombie still attached.

The very thrill that had once brought her joy now became the source of her impending collision. When she crash-landed, the rotter let go and went tumbling down a bank.

Brushing off debris, she scanned the area and noted no other biters. Making a mad rush for the elevator to take her back up, she pushed the button and ascended to the summit.

She emerged from the vertical transport and discovered she wasn't alone. Kane was shambling about, and upon hearing her, he made a lunge for her. His once-familiar features distorted into a grotesque visage of hunger, his outstretched arms reaching menacingly toward her. With a surge of energy, she darted back into the lift, her fingers trembling as she jabbed at the down button, desperate for escape.

Yet, her hopes were dashed as it remained stationary, defying her urgent commands. Puzzled, she peered upward only to gasp in horror as her eyes fell on the source of the obstruction. Two ravenous zombies, their decayed limbs gnarled around the cables, had entangled themselves in a macabre embrace, rendering the mechanism utterly useless.

Without any climbing gear to scale the imposing mountain above her and no visible means of descent, she racked her brain until inspiration struck—she would bungee her way down.

Persistent in his pursuit, Kane stumbled to the platform's edge, his black eyes fixed on her with greedy hunger. With an inherent impulse for survival kicking in, Yara's muscles tensed, her senses sharpening as a rush of adrenaline surged through her veins. Every fiber of her being screamed for action, urging her to find a way out of the perilous situation unfolding before her. She searched frantically for a way to fend off the approaching threat.

Spotting a loose rock nearby, she seized it with tremulous hands and hurled it at him with all her strength. The projectile struck him square in the chest, causing him to stumble backward momentarily. Seizing the opportunity, she lunged forward and executed a powerful kick to his midsection, making him teeter dangerously close to the edge of the cliff.

With a final desperate push, she delivered another forceful blow, sending him tumbling over the ledge with a guttural howl. She gazed breathlessly as he plummeted downward, disappearing from view amidst a cloud of dust and debris, and a sense of relief washed over her as she realized she had narrowly escaped the clutches of the undead.

With him dispatched, Yara hurriedly made her way to the platform, her heart thudding with a combination of fear and perseverance. Fumbling with shaking fingers, she secured the cord to her ankles, her urgency overriding any semblance of caution. Disregarding the customary safety checks in her panicked state, she drew in a shaky breath and flung herself over the edge, just as another rotter was making its reach for her.

As she plummeted toward the ground, a sinking realization dawned upon her—she had neglected to adjust the bungee strap for her height and weight. The earth rushed up to meet her with alarming speed, and she landed with a bone-jarring thud, the impact shattering her legs on contact with the unforgiving rocky terrain. Agony lanced through her body as shockwaves of pain shot up her back, leaving her incapacitated and helpless.

Thrown into the air by the recoil of the line, Yara crashed back down to the surface, her limbs limp and unresponsive. With the elastic rope coming to a sudden halt, she found herself lying defenseless amidst a group of oncoming biters, her inability to move sealing her fate.

As the undead closed in around her, Yara's mind raced with regretful thoughts. "If only I had taken the time to adjust the cord for my height and weight," she lamented, her last moments tinged with the bitter aftertaste of missed opportunities and futile wishes for a different outcome.

Zombie Music Trivia: Round 3

1. Which Misfits song features the lyrics "Zombie, zombie, zombie, ooh"?
2. Who released the song "Zombie Dance" in 1977?
3. What is the name of the American rock band known for their song "Zombie Slide"?
4. Which Alice Cooper album features the song "Zombie Dance"?
5. Who released the song "Zombie Zoo" in 1989?
6. What is the name of the American metalcore band known for their song "Zombie EP"?
7. Which Primus album features the song "Coattails of a Dead Man" with zombie-themed lyrics?

Answers on next page.

1. "Astro Zombies"
2. The Cramps
3. Dr. Steel
4. "Constrictor"
5. Tom Petty
6. The Devil Wears Prada
7. "Antipop"

Chapter 38

Spaceflight Engineer Leo Stevens had dedicated his life to the pursuit of space exploration, and his ultimate dream was to set foot on the moon. After years of rigorous training, he found himself strapped into the spaceship alongside a seasoned crew of four, each member representing the pinnacle of human achievement in their respective fields. As the final countdown echoed through the cockpit, he experienced a surge of euphoria coursing through his veins.

The moment of liftoff was a racket of roaring engines and vibrating metal, the sheer power of the spacecraft propelling them upward with an otherworldly force. His heart pounded in rhythm with the thrumming of the machinery. The clamor of sound filled his ears as they pierced through Earth's atmosphere and into the vastness of space.

As they journeyed further from Earth, with the expanse of space stretching out before them like an endless ocean of stars, Leo's excitement intensified. Then, as they breached orbit and ventured deeper into the cosmos, a shadow fell over the crew. One by one, they succumbed to an unknown illness, their once vibrant faces now pale and drawn with fever. Leo witnessed his comrades writhe in agony, the sickly sweet stench of sickness permeating the confined area of the spacecraft.

Despite his growing concern, he focused on his duties, attempting to maintain a sense of normalcy amidst the chaos unfolding around him. But as the hours stretched into an agonizing blur, it became apparent that their situation was dire. The crew's condition deteriorated rapidly, their bodies racked with violent tremors and convulsions that left him feeling helpless and alone.

Then, as they neared the moon's orbit, the true horror of their predicament revealed itself. One by one, his crewmates underwent a repulsive transformation, their once-human forms contorting into something monstrous and unrecognizable. Leo's stomach churned as he watched in shock, the acrid scent of fear mingling with the metallic taste of bile rising in his throat.

Desperate to escape the nightmare unfolding before him, he retreated to the engineering area of the spacecraft, his hands shaking as he struggled to comprehend the gravity of their situation. With each passing moment, the deafening roar of his racing heartbeat filled his ears, drowning out the distant hum of the ship's engines as they hurtled toward their target.

As the ship began its descent to the moon's surface, Leo's mind raced with a frantic urgency, his senses overwhelmed by the surreal spectacle facing him. An unpleasant glare of sunlight reflected off the lunar landscape, casting long shadows across the barren terrain as they flew to their final destination.

With a jarring impact, the spacecraft touched down, sending shockwaves rippling through his body as he struggled to maintain his footing. The steel jangle of aerospace-grade aluminum against rock reverberated through the cabin. The harsh noise echoed in his ears as he fought to regain his composure.

Despite the chaos unfolding around him, Leo forced himself to focus, his hands moving with practiced precision as he flicked switches, powered down the craft, and donned a spacesuit. With a hiss of released air, the doors of the ship swung open, revealing the desolate landscape spreading out in front of him.

Stepping out onto the lunar surface, with a sense of profound isolation washing over him, he beheld the boundless scope of the celestial wasteland stretching out before him like an alien environment. With the infected crew hot on his heels, he knew that his only chance of survival lay in leading them away from the spaceship and toward the farthest reaches of the moon.

Every step was like an eternity as he bounded across the rugged terrain in the low gravity. The undead squad drew closer, their twisted forms silhouetted against the stark lunar surroundings as they pursued him with determined persistence.

With his oxygen level steadily dwindling and no means of replenishing it, he sensed the weight of his predicament pressing down on him like the crushing embrace of gravity itself. Inside his spacesuit, the incessant beep of the air supply alarm served as a haunting reminder of his impending doom, each shrill sound cutting through the silence like a knife.

Glancing back at the zombified figures of his teammates, their once-familiar faces now twisted into misshapen masks of decay, a shiver of dread coursed through him. In slow, meandering motions, they lurched forward, their ragged breaths emerging as eerie groans that raised the hairs on the back of his neck.

With his options dwindling, Leo's mind raced, searching for a way to evade his undead pursuers. Remembering the unique properties of the moon's gravity, he stood poised like a football player, his muscles tense with anticipation. As the infected crew drew closer, he waited until the very last second before springing into action.

With a powerful leap, Leo soared through the air, his heart pounding in his chest as he sailed over the heads of his zombie enemies. Landing with a resounding thud, he turned to face them, only to find them mimicking his every move with unnerving precision. It was like a macabre game of leapfrog, each jump bringing him nearer to the edge of despair.

Frustration boiled over as he struggled to outmaneuver his relentless pursuers, their decomposing forms closing in faster by the second. With a final desperate leap, he soared into the air, only to collide with one of the creatures mid-flight.

The impact sent him spiraling out of control, his body tumbling in a dizzying display of pandemonium. As he spun and rolled, the darkness of the lunar landscape whirled around him, a disorienting blur of movement and confusion.

Through the haze of vertigo, nausea held him hostage, the foul taste of bile flooding his mouth as he struggled to regain his bearings. With every revolution, his helmet filled with regurgitated vomit, the unpleasant scent mingling with the stale air of his suit.

Leo kept rolling with no way to stop his momentum. Each time he came within sight of the spaceship, it was out of focus. Despair flooded his senses as he continued to spiral further away from it, caught in the endless spin. Trapped in this constant whirl, a vortex rippled through his system as he experienced motion sickness that refused to abate. He came to the understanding that he was forever marooned in the vast emptiness of space, with no means of reaching the ship.

In the silent infinity of the cosmos, Leo wished for the release of a meteor shower to end his torment, but none came. Only the cold embrace of the empty void awaited him as his air ran out.

Zombie Poems: 3

Flamboyant hair, a signature style,
Forget blending in, let's stand out awhile.
No subtlety for me, just a colorful do,
"Zombies, check out this hair!" my bold debut.

***

A neon "Buffet - Happy Hour" sign,
Forget stealthy escapes, let's dine and wine.
No survival skills, just a feast and cheer,
"Zombies, the buffet's open!" my end is near.

***

A zombie-themed circus, a grand affair,
Forget caution, let's put on a scare.
No safety nets, just laughter and dread,
"Welcome, zombies, to the circus!" my circus undead.

***

Glow-in-the-dark stickers on shelter's wall,
Forget camouflage, let's shine through it all.
No hidden refuge, just a radiant gleam,
"Zombies, my hideout's aglow!" my misguided dream.

Chapter 39

As Harry sprinted through the desolate streets, panic gripped him as he pondered his current predicament. At forty-two, he had never anticipated his midlife crisis taking the form of a desperate bid for survival against the undead. He had imagined it involving a sports car or perhaps some ill-advised tattoos.

However, in the face of the zombie apocalypse, he found himself rapidly becoming the villain. He used other humans as shields by shoving them into the path of oncoming hordes, caring only about his own life regardless of the cost.

With a horde of zombies chasing him, Harry spotted two young men attempting to outrun the revenants. "Hey, you guys! Come with me. I'll take you to safety!" he shouted. The two males eagerly followed his lead, trusting him to guide them to sanctuary. Yet, as they drew near, gasping for breath, he seized the moment and callously shoved them into the waiting arms of the hungry rotters. Their screams of being betrayed echoed behind him as he continued on, heedless of their fate.

Navigating through the infected streets, he glimpsed the towering gates of a zoo in the distance. It appeared like the perfect refuge to regroup, replenish supplies, and formulate a new plan. As he dashed toward the entrance, a woman emerged, providing him with the opportunity to divert the fast-approaching zombies' attention. Without hesitation, he thrust her at the encroaching horde, buying precious moments to evade their grasp.

Running through the pathways, he found himself at a dead end, the undead closing in from all sides. With no human shields left to protect him, he faced a critical decision. Confront the oncoming swarm head-on or take a leap of faith into the nearest enclosure. Unfazed by the thought of exploiting the zoo's inhabitants for his own survival, he chose the latter.

Bounding over the railings, he plummeted twenty feet into the gorilla pen below. Before his descent, he made sure to draw the attention of the pursuing creatures, ensuring they followed him into the compound. As the ghouls crashed into the pit after him, he scanned his surroundings and spotted a lone silverback. Using the ape as a distraction, he deftly maneuvered around the boundary, leading the infected zombies into the path of the powerful ape.

Without hesitation, the primate sprang into action, joined by several others, tearing into the flesh-eaters with primal ferocity. Seizing the opportunity amidst the chaos, Harry swiftly navigated his way into the indoor enclosure, utilizing it as his means of escape from the unstoppable chase of the undead. He swaggered into the entrance of the passageway, his confidence masking the trepidation churning within.

Straightening his shoulders, he viewed the exit and made a quick dash across the well-worn passage where zookeepers typically entered and exited. To his dismay, he found the gate securely locked from the outside. Cursing under his breath, he thrust his hand through the grates, touching the cold metal of the lock. With gritted teeth, he twisted and pulled, his fingers straining against the stubborn mechanism. Fuming at the realization that it was padlocked, he withdrew his digits, frustration boiling inside him as he scanned the perimeter for another escape route.

The enclosure near him was a lush replica of a tropical rainforest, meticulously designed to mimic the gorillas' natural habitat. Towering trees, their branches adorned with thick foliage, cast dappled shadows across the verdant ground below. Robust vines snaked their way around sturdy trunks, providing ample opportunities for the primates to swing and climb. The air was alive with the melody of the jungle. The chorus of birdcalls and rustling leaves adding to the immersive experience of the simulated ecosystem.

His eyes scanned the surroundings for any possible means of egress. He spotted a promising area where a tree near the fence looked scalable. Determination flared within him as he approached, his gaze fixed on his potential route to freedom. With agile movements, he began to scale the bark, his fingers gripping the textured exterior as he ascended. However, just as he neared the top, his foot slipped on a moss-covered branch and he tumbled backward, landing with an embarrassing thud.

Undeterred by the setback, he dusted himself off and resolved to try again. With renewed commitment, he planted his feet firmly on the tree trunk and resumed his ascent. Yet, despite his efforts, he struggled to find purchase on the slick surface, his muscles straining with the exertion. —Before he could make another attempt, his gaze was drawn to a magnificent sight nearby—the imposing figure of a silverback, its powerful form radiating an aura of authority.

In the heart of the enclosure, a hand-painted oversized tire lay abandoned amidst the lush foliage, its vibrant colors standing out against the verdant backdrop. Surrounding it were an array of toys scattered about, their bright hues peeking through the flora. Swinging ropes hung from sturdy branches, swaying gently in the breeze and beckoning the gorillas to partake in their playful antics.

Harry's eyes darted around the scene, frantically searching for a means of defense in the middle of the tranquil playground. His gaze fell on a large ball nestled among the greenery, a glimmer of hope igniting within him. With sweaty hands, he picked it up, its smooth surface slick with dew, and he hurled it at the approaching gorilla with all his might.

With a bang, the ball collided with the primate, only to be brushed away by the primate's lazy swipe. Undeterred, his heart raced as he scanned the area for another escape route, only to be met with the deep hoot of another ape emerging from the shadows. Upon hearing the sound of thumping, he shifted his gaze toward the larger one. Witnessing its huffing and chest-beating, Harry's hairs stood on end.

With a plunging sensation of dread, he realized he was trapped between two intimidating predators. When they bared their teeth, he could see how sharp they were, and how they looked against the backdrop of dark gums. The long and pointed canines added to the daunting appearance. He paled, fear surging through his veins like a torrent of icy water and chilling him to the core. Anguish flooded through him as he once more attempted to scale the tree, but the slick bark offered no purchase, sending him tumbling back to the ground in defeat.

As the gorillas closed in, their imposing figures casting murky silhouettes over him, Harry's breath caught in his throat. In a final, desperate gambit, he unleashed a blood-curdling scream, hoping against hope to attract the attention of close zombies. But his plea fell on deaf ears as the ghouls remained absent, leaving him to face his impending doom alone.

With resignation weighing heavily on his shoulders, Harry braced himself for the inevitable onslaught, his quivering body pressed on the bark of the tree. The noise of the primates' approach filled the air, their deep grunts and hoots growing louder with each passing moment, signaling the swift arrival of his demise.

Zombie Music Trivia: Round 4

1. Who released the song "Zombie Delight" in 2005?
2. What is the name of the American thrash metal band known for their song "Zombie Attack"?
3. Which Guaraldi album features the song "Zombie's Lament"?
4. Who released the song "Zombie Prostitute" in 2007?
5. What is the name of the American punk band known for their song "Zombie Dance Party"?
6. Which Faith No More album features the song "Zombie Eaters"?
7. Who released the song "Zombies Ate Her Brain" in 2006?

Answers on next page.

1. Buck 65
2. Tankard
3. "The Eclectic Mind Of"
4. Voltaire
5. The Creepshow
6. "The Real Thing"
7. The Creepshow

Chapter 40

Miguel, fueled by bravado and a false sense of invincibility, armed himself with makeshift weapons cobbled together from items acquired within the prison. Despite ample opportunities to leave unscathed, he was dead set on staying. His plan? Straightforward—take on the zombie horde head-on and show them the true meaning of a good ol' brawl.

As he burst into the corridor, the zombies turned their attention to him. His first swing with a crudely fashioned pipe connected with a zombie's head, sending it sprawling to the floor. In that brief moment, he experienced a surge of excitement, convinced that he could single-handedly take on the undead onslaught.

The narrow confines of the prison hallway were about as accommodating to Miguel's brawling style as a cat in a room full of rocking chairs. Deadheads approached from all sides, surrounding him with a nightmarish horde of rotters. The flickering lights overhead cast unsettling silhouettes on the cold, damp walls as he braced for the impending attack. The stench of decay mixed with the musty odor of the penitentiary created a nauseating atmosphere that only ignited his commitment.

With a primal scream, he launched into the fray, his fists becoming a blur of furious strikes. Every punch landed with a sickening squelch as his knuckles made contact with the rotting flesh of the undead. He experienced the sensation of his fist sinking into the soft, decaying tissue. The cold, clammy texture spurred him to keep going.

As he fought, his eyes caught sight of a zombie's chest, its innards visible through its thin, translucent skin. With each powerful blow, he witnessed in grim fascination as its heart sucked inward, only to spring back like a rubber band, beating behind decomposing ribs that acted like a Venus flytrap.

Blood sprayed across his face and the floor as he battled tooth and nail. With no more improvised weapons, he used his body as a weapon against the encroaching tide of death. The distant clatter of metal bars and inmate shouts created a disorder that rippled through the prison walls. In this morbid ballet of brutality, he fought not only for his own survival but also to prove his strength in facing the zombies, disregarding any chance to escape the suffocating darkness of the prison's fortress.

Miguel swung wildly, dealing blows to the infected, but for every zombie he incapacitated, two more emerged like unwanted party guests crashing through the door. Swamped by sheer numbers, his aggressive fighting style unleashed a torrent of strikes, each punch powered by the raw ferocity of a street fighter, unwilling to give up.

A rotter lunged at him, its jaws snapping hungrily. With lightning reflexes, he sidestepped and delivered a devastating roundhouse kick to its decaying skull. The force of the blow sent the creature's head spinning off its shoulders in a sickening spray of claret and gore that painted the ground crimson.

A particularly large living dead specimen barreled toward him, its arms outstretched like claws. Miguel braced himself and met the creature head-on, driving his shoulder into its chest with all the power he could muster. There was a nauseating crunch as brittle bones snapped under the impact, the zombie's howl of pain mingling with his own grunts of exertion.

Blood trickled from a gash on his forehead, mixing with sweat as it dripped down his face. His heart pounded in his ears, the rhythm matching the frenzied chaos of the battle raging around him. Each breath felt like fire in his lungs, but still, he pressed on, fueled by sheer determination and the will to survive.

In his fervor, adrenaline coursing through his veins like wildfire, his movements became a whirlwind of violence and urgency. With a fierce will burning in his eyes, he attempted a fancy spinning kick, a move that would have made Bruce Lee nod in approval. His leg shot out with lightning speed, aimed for the nearest revenant's decaying skull, but the slick floor betrayed him.

Mid-spin, his foot slipped on a patch of spilled blood, sending him careening off-balance. Time seemed to slow as he sensed his body tilting precariously, his arms windmilling in an attempt to regain control. With a jarring thud, he landed flat on his back. The impact knocked the wind out of him, and stars danced in his vision.

Like a stranded turtle, he lay there for a moment, dazed and disoriented, the taste of defeat bitter on his tongue. But he refused to stay down and his natural-born killer instincts kicked into overdrive. With a grunt of effort, he attempted to push himself upright, only to find his progress hindered by the weight of his own body.

In his haste, he thrashed about, limbs floundering wildly in a desperate bid for freedom. And then, in a stroke of cruel irony, karma intervened once more. As he struggled to rise, his head collided with the chest of a nearby zombie, stunning them both with the impact. For a fleeting moment, they remained locked in a chilling embrace, his skull ringing from the force of the blow while the corpse appeared stunned by the unexpected collision.

Miguel's will to survive burned bright. With a groan of exertion, he broke free from the creature's grasp, scrambling to his feet with renewed forcefulness. He executed a move that could have been in a Buster Keaton movie. Thinking he could outmaneuver the deadheads, he endeavored a daring leapfrog over a group of them, only to land in the middle of them, surrounded and looking more like a human game of Twister than a fearsome fighter.

Desperate to regain control of the situation, he tried to channel his inner ninja and execute a stealthy disappearing act. Regret colored his attempt at stealth, which was about as subtle as a hardened criminal trying to outrun the cops with no legs. He tripped over his own feet, crashing into a pile of discarded prison mattresses with a resounding bang that echoed through the passage.

By this point, his bravado had evaporated like a puddle in the desert, leaving behind a bewildered and slightly bruised would-be hero. As he faced down the relentless horde of rotters, he couldn't help but wonder if perhaps he had underestimated the gravity of the situation or overestimated his own abilities.

But there was no time for self-reflection. With a resigned sigh and a muttered curse at his own foolishness, he squared his shoulders and prepared to face whatever came his way. Except there was no preparedness for what came next. A living dead one clamped onto Miguel's arm, and another sank its teeth into his leg, treating him like a tasty buffet at a zombie banquet.

Freeing himself from the biters, he continued to fight, using his remaining strength to land punches and kicks with all the grace of a drunken octopus trying to play the bagpipes. His confidence wavered, with the onslaught proving too much for even his reckless abandon.

In a final act of defiance, he swung his fist one last time, only to be tackled to the ground by a group of undead. The chaotic brawl ended in a pile of limbs and gnashing teeth. Miguel's boldness crumbled in the face of overwhelming odds.

Zombie Poems: 4

Neon skywriting, announcing my stay,
Forget secrecy, let's light up the way.
No subtlety for me, just a sky-high display,
"Zombies, here I am!" my skywriting dismay.

***

Zombie-themed poetry, a lyrical rhyme,
Forget survival tips, let's jest through time.
No serious tone, just laughter and zest,
"Zombies, applaud my rhymes!" my poetic unrest.

***

A zombie-themed wedding, vows to decay,
Forget solemnity, let's laugh our way.
No serious promises, just undead bliss,
"Zombies, join the union!" my nuptial abyss.

***

Karaoke anthems in the midst of the swarm,
Forget silence, let's sing and perform.
No stealth for me, just a vocal display,
"Zombies, enjoy the melody!" my song in dismay.

Chapter 41

Within the enclosed confines of the university dormitory's narrow corridors, Elena, a science professor with a crippling fear of tight spaces, found herself crawling into a duct under protest, hoping to evade the undead. With cautious and calculated movements, she ventured into the complex passages.

In the low-lit air vent, with whole-body tremors, she maneuvered through the cramped space, her breaths shallow and labored. With each inch she crawled, the claustrophobic nightmare tightened its grip around her, suffocating her with an invisible weight. The dread that haunted her now became a tangible force, pressing down on her chest and squeezing her lungs tight.

She lay flat on her stomach, the cold metallic floor touching her, her breath short and rapid. The sound of groaning zombies reverberated through the thin veil of metal separating her from the undead horde below, intensifying her fear.

Every muscle in her body tensed as she clenched her jaw, willing herself to remain still. There was barely enough room for her to put her hands over her head. Her fingers brushed against the rough surface of the vent. She could feel the sweat penetrating her shirt, mingling with the grime and dust of the confined passage.

With painstaking slowness, Elena inched forward in a snake-like slither, her movements constrained by the narrowness of the duct. Each movement sent a jolt of panic through her, her breath hitching in her throat. Her heart raced, its frantic beats matching the rhythm of her labored breathing.

The air grew thick and oppressive, suffocating her as she struggled to push through the tight space. Beads of sweat trickled down her brow, stinging her eyes as she fought to control her rising fear. Her heartbeat began to hammer against her ribcage, threatening to burst from her chest as she wrestled to maintain her composure.

In the darkness of the vent, Elana's anxiety started to overpower her. Every creak and groan of the metal walls set her nerves on edge. She closed her eyes, willing herself to focus on her breathing, to block out the overwhelming dread that threatened to consume her.

As she crept further into the conduit, a rodent darted past her, its tiny feet skittering over her shoe, causing her to freeze and close her eyes in terror. When she dared to blink them open, she was face to face with a large rat, its beady eyes staring back at her. The bristles of its fur brushed next to her nose. A scream lodged in her throat, but she bit it back, forcing herself to remember a childhood memory—one that made her forget about the vermin.

She remembered the time when she and her brother had decided to create a homemade rocket using their father's old firecrackers. They planned the launch, setting up a launchpad in the backyard. With eagerness, they counted down to blast-off.

But as soon as they ignited the fireworks, instead of soaring into the sky, their spaceship careened off course, crashing into the neighbor's fence and sending the local birds scattering in alarm. The sight of their failed liftoff left them in fits of laughter, rolling on the grass with tears streaming down their faces.

The memory of their missile fiasco flooded back to her, and despite the tense situation she found herself in, she couldn't help but laugh at it, grateful for the distraction. The image of her brother's shocked expression was sufficient to bring a smile to her face, easing the tension of the moment.

With a slight giggle, she glanced at the rat in front of her and imagined it wearing a tiny astronaut helmet, preparing for a disastrous rocket launch of its own. Amused by the mental picture, she suddenly screwed up her face and tightened every muscle as the rodent twitched. It then climbed over her arm and over her head, down her back, and vanished somewhere behind her. Without warning, her right calf began to spasm as a cramp took her hostage. She couldn't move to relieve it. All she could do was wait it out in agony. When it finally abated, she released her held breath, realizing she had been holding it throughout the ordeal.

Moments later, a spider crawled across her hand and she let out a startled yelp, swatting at it with frantic slaps. She grimaced as she wiped away the cobwebs it left. As she struggled to compose herself, her heart sank with each dwindling second. Faced with the sensation of a tunnel constricting around her, squeezing the air from her lungs, she clawed at the walls in desperation. She sought relief from the suffocating pressure but found none. With every passing moment, the darkness appeared to close in on her, and she feared she would never escape the frightening, cramped situation.

Arm-over-arm in a commando crawl, she traversed the restrictive vent. All of a sudden, with a resounding clang, the panel beneath her collapsed, sending her crashing down onto a huddle of ghouls below. The impact jolted the breath from her lungs. But by sheer luck, the undead mass absorbed much of the force, sparing her from any broken bones.

Regaining her composure, she scrambled to her feet and reached for the door of the room she had fallen into. Surveying her surroundings, she realized she was in the university's laundry facility. With the entrance obstructed by more zombies, she frantically sought a spot to hide.

Her eyes landed on an industrial-sized dryer looming in the corner. With no time to spare, she hurried over and hoisted herself inside, yanking the heavy door closed behind her with a loud bang. Through the distorted window on the appliance, resembling the lens of a fly, she could make out the undead as they approached her hiding place.

Crouched in the cramped space, Elena's panting came in short gasps as she hoped they couldn't get to her. But before she could catch her breath, the walkers knew where she was, their guttural moans growing louder with each uncoordinated movement. In their frenzied attempt to reach her, they repeatedly slammed into the metal sides of the dryer, inadvertently setting it in motion.

As the machine roared to life, Elena was tossed about like a ragdoll inside the tumbling drum. Intense heat quickly enveloped her, sending waves of discomfort through her body. She struggled to kick the door open. The extreme swelter from the dryer's interior began to sear her skin, causing unbearable pain. The metallic walls around her radiated like an inferno, and she could feel herself burning from the outside in. But the worst was yet to come.

With each passing second, the temperature continued to climb, and soon Elena experienced being cooked alive from within. The scorching air filled her lungs, making it difficult to breathe, while her internal organs protested against the relentless heat.

Desperation engulfed her as she realized the horrifying truth—she was sizzling, internally and externally—trapped in this fiery hell with no hope of rescue. As flames licked at her skin and their intensity threatened to consume her, she became overwhelmed by excruciating pain. She closed her eyes, imprisoned in an industrial dryer, her screams silenced by the deafening noise of the inferno.

The rotting corpses stood motionless, their vacant expressions fixed on the spinning drum with no clue on how to reach their meal.

Zombie Music Trivia: Round 5

1. What is the name of the American metal band known for their song "Zombie Ritual"?
2. Which The Cramps album features the song "Zombie Dance"?
3. Who released the song "Zombie Stomp" in 2008?
4. What is the name of the American rock band known for their song "Zombie Honeymoon"?
5. Which Your Favorite Martian album features the song "Zombie Love Song"?
6. Who released the song "Zombie Love Song" in 2011?
7. What is the name of the American musician known for his song "Zombie Honeymoon"?
8. Which Creepshow album features the song "Zombie Stomp"?

Answers on next page.

1. Death
2. "Songs the Lord Taught Us"
3. The Creepshow
4. The Honorary Title
5. "Your Favorite Martian"
6. Your Favorite Martian
7. The Honorary Title
8. "Run for Your Life"

Chapter 42

During the zombie apocalypse, Gertrude, a makeup artist with a knack for special effects, found solace in her craft. With meticulous attention to detail, she blended shades of decay and rot onto her skin to mimic the grotesque appearance of the walking dead. Using spilled blood from a rotter, she smeared it over her clothing, her flesh, and in her hair. She transformed her image into that of a convincing member of the undead. Not only did she evade the monsters, but she also merged in with their ranks, becoming indistinguishable from the rotting horde.

As she moved among the zombies, her once-human features obscured by layers of cosmetics, she drew the gaze of the survivors. Navigating through the throngs of the rotters, her movements mirrored those of the creatures surrounding her. Suddenly, chaos erupted as a group of individuals opened fire on the swarm. Bullets whizzed through the air, tearing through decaying flesh and sending showers of blood and gore over her and in all directions. Gertrude dove for cover, her heart racing as she narrowly escaped a volley of gunfire.

Amidst the disorder, she struggled to maintain her composure, her breath coming in shallow gasps as she pressed her body against the cold concrete wall of a nearby building. The sounds of screams and gunshots echoed around her, merging with the rough moans of the undead.

Gertrude's fear threatened to consume her as she realized that one wrong move, one misplaced step, could mean the difference between life and death, as she would be mistaken for one of the deadheads. She cursed herself for the reckless gamble she had taken, masquerading as one of the zombies in a desperate bid to survive. Despite the danger, she couldn't deny the twisted thrill that surged through her veins as she danced on the edge. There was something exhilarating about the risk, about the adrenaline-fueled rush of escaping the clutches of the undead.

As the gunfire subsided and the survivors moved on, leaving behind a trail of destruction and mortality, Gertrude emerged from her hiding spot, her body drenched in gore. She trembled with excitement and fear. The surge coursing through her was intoxicating, mixing with the palpable sense of relief that she had once again escaped death's grasp. Yet, beneath the surface, a gnawing uncertainty lingered. The line between survival and moral compromise blurred further, thrusting her into a tumultuous struggle with the weight of her choices.

She melted back into the ranks of the undead, convinced she was doing the right thing to survive. The haunting screams of the survivors and the grunts of the deadheads were a grim reminder of the harsh reality of their existence. Gertrude pushed aside the lingering doubts, burying them deep within as she focused on the task at hand—blending in with the zombies, a silent fake predator among the horde.

In her fervent determination to prevail, she failed to look where she was stepping and stumbled over a smoldering, fallen corpse. The searing heat of the charred remains scorched her skin, sending a jolt of pain coursing through her body as she struggled to regain her balance. She glanced up as a flaming bottle landed nearby her. Getting to her feet, she veered toward another group of rotters, avoiding the Molotov cocktails.

Together with the crowd she had mingled with, they moved with eerie coordination, navigating through the fiery onslaught unscathed. They managed to evade being burned to a crisp, disappearing into the darkness of the night as the flames raged on, leaving behind only the lingering scent of smoke and destruction. Her superficial burns stung and her head ached, yet she found deep down the ability to keep going.

Days blurred into nights, and she soon realized the perils of masquerading as one of the infected. Caught between the gnashing teeth of the zombies and trigger-happy survivors, she faced a crucial decision. Should she risk removing her makeup and face the wrath of both factions, or attempt to navigate through the end of the world and evade relentless attacks from either side?

Her indecision proved disadvantageous as a lone survivor, mistaking her for a real zombie, unleashed a flurry of arrows in her direction. With a shriek, she bolted, narrowly avoiding becoming a pincushion. Despite her fear of attracting attention, she couldn't help but yell out in pain as an arrow found its mark in her backside, further complicating her predicament. With the gusto of a wrestler, she pulled it out, rubbed herself down, and carried on. Her injury added to her disguise, as now she hobbled.

While she navigated within the horde, she encountered a desperate group of housewives who had clad themselves in armor fashioned from kitchen utensils, wielding oversized spatulas, ladles, and rolling pins. With a battle cry of "Dinner's served!"—which sounded like a cooking show catchphrase—they charged into the swarm of zombies.

Gertrude couldn't help but stifle a laugh as she witnessed the surreal sight unfold before her eyes. She dodged flying frying pans and ducked when an extra-large soup pot swung too close to her head. In the distance, great booming vibrations reached her ears, and she realized that the undead appeared attracted to the ruckus, drawn to the noise like moths to a flame. The housewives retreated when the deadheads became distracted by the explosive sounds. She mingled back within the group of rotters, utilizing her zombified look.

Traversing the wasteland, she maintained her decomposing facade, blending among the walkers. However, her realistic appearance proved to be a double-edged sword as she stumbled upon a heavily fortified city area, brimming with specialized soldiers armed to the teeth and ready to exterminate the revenant threat.

In the pandemonium of explosions and gunfire, Gertrude's attempts to signal her humanness to the military forces was futile. Jumping up and down in a desperate bid for recognition only drew more suspicion. Her frantic actions to remove her makeup, intended to reveal her humanity, only succeeded in smudging her face more. This accentuated her corpse-like appearance, further complicating her predicament.

Avoiding the path of approaching tanks, her hopes of survival were dashed as a sharp pain tore through her abdomen, a bullet sealing her fate in a tragic finale. With a gut-wrenching realization, Gertrude collapsed to the ground, clutching her stomach in agony as the weight of her deeds came crashing down upon her.

As she lay there, her lifeblood seeping from the wound, she couldn't help but curse her decision to dabble in undead aesthetics. But before she could grasp the full extent of her folly, a nearby zombie, drawn by the scent of blood, lunged towards her fading form. With a sickening crunch, it sank its rotting mouth into her legs, tearing away flesh in a gruesome feast.

Another creature joined in, gnashing its teeth into her arm, adding to the torment of her final moments. As the zombies feasted upon her dying corpse,

Gertrude's mind clouded with the bitter irony of her demise. Not only had she been mistaken for one of the rotters by humans, but now she was being devoured by the very creatures she had sought to emulate.

Zombie Poems: 5

A neon "Follow Me" sign, shining bright,
Forget subtlety, let's guide them with light.
No cautious steps, just a neon lead,
"Zombies, follow the sign!" my perilous thread.

***

A zombie-themed Olympics, a sporting delight,
Forget survival drills, let's compete in the night.
No focus on safety, just medals and cheer,
"Zombies, let the games begin!" my game of fear.

***

A zombie-themed prom, dancing undead,
Forget quiet escapes, let's party instead.
No hushed whispers, just music and sway,
"Zombies, join the dance!" my promenade astray.

***

Unicycle rides in a world gone mad,
Forget practicality, let's look quite rad.
No sturdy wheels, just balancing grace,
"Zombies, check my skill!" my precarious embrace.

Chapter 43

Bea, a formidable figure with sinewy muscles and a steely gaze, prowled the deserted streets like a silent sentinel. Her senses were sharp, attuned to the slightest disturbance in the eerie silence that enveloped the desolate landscape. She wasn't your typical survivor, rather a masculine woman with a flair for the dramatic and a penchant for setting up all manner of traps.

The night draped the abandoned town in a shroud of darkness, broken only by the feeble glow of the moon. Amidst the haunting stillness, a faint rustling broke the tranquility. The unmistakable sound of stumbling footsteps followed it, erratic and disjointed, echoing through the hollow corridors of the forsaken community. Bea's muscles tensed as she recognized the telltale signs of the undead drawing near.

From her concealed vantage point atop a dilapidated building, she surveyed the settlement she had claimed as her own. Bea was not just a survivor, she was the master of this domain and the architect of its defenses. Every corner, every alleyway, was a testament to her ingenuity, transformed into a labyrinth of destruction for the unwary dead.

Tripwires crisscrossed the narrow streets like spiderwebs, hidden from view but deadly to the touch. At the slightest misstep, they triggered a cascade of explosions that reduced the undead to nothing more than a cloud of pulverized flesh and bone.

In the shadows of alleyways, pitfalls lay concealed beneath layers of debris, waiting to ensnare the unsuspecting deadheads. One false move and the surface would give way, swallowing the rotters whole as they plummeted into the darkness below.

Everywhere, the very ground under their feet was a treacherous maze of obstacles and snares. Floorboards rigged with camouflaged mechanisms sprang to life with a deafening clang, impaling any unfortunate soul who dared to tread upon them with deadly spikes that rose from the earth like the jaws of a hungry predator.

But perhaps the most ingenious of Bea's creations were the traps that defied gravity itself. Ropes and wires snaked through the air like serpents, their fatal embrace coiling around the ankles of the undead and hoisting them skyward, suspended upside down like grotesque mannequins.

As the first of the zombies stumbled into her meticulously laid snares, they met their demise with a clamor of screams and clattering metal. Each trap sprung into action with lethal precision, ensnaring the corpse in a web of death from which there was no escape.

Through it all, Bea surveyed everything from her perch atop the crumbling remains of a once-grand building, her eyes gleaming with a fierce determination. She was the queen of this forsaken kingdom, the master of trickery who had turned an abandoned village into a fortress of fatality. And as the night wore on, she knew that her domain would remain secure, protected by the lethal ingenuity of her designs.

As dusk settled like a heavy curtain, she spotted her first target of the evening—a lone zombie stumbling through the debris. With a smirk, she activated her device, a tripwire connected to a net. The infected one lumbered forward, causing the wire to activate and becoming entangled in the mesh. But what caught her attention was not the ghoul's predicament, but its comical attempts to free itself. With arms thrashing and legs kicking, it resembled a tangled dummy, its hollow struggles only serving to entangle it further.

Smirking, she dispatched the trapped corpse with a swift blow to the head, relishing the satisfaction of a successful quest. She returned to her hideout to build more contraptions. A few days went by devoid of any biters wandering in. During her daily scouting, she came across some creatures that had been caught in her snares, killing each and then taking a five-minute break before carrying on with the hunt.

But her work was far from over. Moving deeper into her domain, she spotted a group of rotters meandering without purpose. This time, she opted for a more elaborate trap. A pitfall disguised beneath a layer of leaves and branches. With careful precision, she lured them toward the snare, watching with glee as they stumbled into the pit one by one, impaling themselves on the sharpened stakes at the bottom.

What tickled her funny bone was the sight of them squirming and wriggling while impaled. Their attempts to break free resembled fish flopping around out of water, with uncoordinated movements and contorted rotting limbs provoking a bubbling rise of giggles from deep within her. Halting her laughter, she moved in to finish them off, pausing to admire her handiwork. Once she ensured they were double-dead, she advanced onward.

Overflowing with confidence, she skillfully maneuvered through her traps, relishing the chase like a battle-hardened warrior. As she strode through the overgrown foliage, her focus fixed on the path ahead, a sudden crackling sound shattered the eerie silence. Before she could react, the ground beneath her feet gave way, sending her tumbling into the darkness below.

The abruptness of her fall jolted her body with stabbing pain, but she shook it off with a grunt, her sturdy frame absorbing the impact. Grimacing, battered, and bruised, she brushed herself off, determined to get out. She cursed aloud at her own foolishness, realizing too late the gravity of her mistake.

She let out a low growl of frustration, then delivered a sharp slap to her cheeks, dumbfounded by her own oversight. How could she have prowled through the foliage without checking for signs of her own snares, only to foolishly step on one of her own contraptions?

Stunned and disoriented, she fought to regain her footing as the realization dawned upon her. She was now ensnared, a prisoner of her own design. With a deep groan of exasperation, she surveyed her surroundings, seeking a means of escape.

The walls of the pit were smooth and unyielding, offering no handholds or footholds to get out. Despite her usual stoicism, a flicker of vulnerability seeped through her hardened exterior as she grappled with the magnitude of her predicament.

Trapped like a warrior in her own fortress, she cursed her luck and pondered the irony of her situation. As the hours stretched into days, she resigned herself to her fate, knowing that she had met her match in the greatest and unlikeliest of opponents—none other than her own cleverness. And so, with a heavy heart and a humbled spirit, she awaited oblivion.

Zombie Music Trivia: Round 6

1. Who released the song "Zombie Queen" in 2010?
2. What is the name of the Canadian musician known for his song "Zombie Woof"?
3. Which Laura Shigihara album features the song "Zombies On Your Lawn"?
4. Who released the song "Zombies On Your Lawn" in 2009?
5. What is the name of the American singer-songwriter known for her song "Zombie Song"?
6. Which Dr. Steel album features the song "Zombie Slide"?
7. Who released the song "Zombie Slide" in 2006?

Answers on next page.

1. Ghost
2. Frank Zappa
3. "Plants vs. Zombies Soundtrack"
4. Laura Shigihara
5. Stephanie Mabey
6. "People of Earth"
7. Dr. Steel

Chapter 44

In the post-apocalyptic world, where the undead roamed without restraint and survival was paramount, there was one woman who had an unconventional approach to matters of the heart—Joanne, a plucky twenty-something with a fondness for adventure and a crush on a particularly dashing zombie.

It all started one fateful day when she stumbled upon Zed while scavenging for supplies in an abandoned supermarket. There he was, shambling with an uneven gait down the canned goods aisle, his decaying flesh and vacant stare doing nothing to dampen Joanne's enthusiasm. With a flutter of excitement, she decided then and there that he would be hers.

Equipped with nothing but perseverance and a length of chain she found in the gardening section, she embarked on her quest to capture the object of her affection. It was a sight to behold as she chased after him, dodging swipes from his rotting limbs and sidestepping his gnashing teeth.

Armed with her trusty steel links, she tried to corral him as he stumbled clumsily through the narrow aisles of the abandoned supermarket. A shopping cart discarded by its previous customer proved to be a hindrance and a barricade as she dodged and weaved, avoiding collisions with him and the rusted metal contraption.

In her urgency, she seized a broomstick from a nearby display, brandishing it like a weapon as she attempted to fend off Zed's feeble attempts to grab at her. With each wild swing, she sent cans of expired tuna flying in all directions, the metallic clang of tin echoing through the empty store as he lurched at her with awkward, grabby hands. His undead moans were drowned out by Joanne's joyous laughter and playful cries of encouragement.

Despite the challenging situation, her dedication never wavered. With a mixture of luck and willpower, she managed to maneuver him into a corner. Whirling her chain through the air like a lasso, she attempted to ensnare her zombie quarry. After an intense struggle back and forth, Joanne emerged victorious, like a seasoned rodeo performer taming a wild bull.

With her leash wrapped securely around Zed's neck, she breathed a sigh of relief and triumph as she bound him to an empty rack before embarking on a scavenger hunt.

She scoured the deserted aisles of the supermarket, her eyes scanning the shelves for the perfect instrument for her unconventional task, bypassing the canned goods and expired snacks. Her focus remained unwavering as she sought out the one item that would fulfill her infatuated desire.

Her heart fluttered like a whimsical butterfly as she rounded a corner and spotted a dusty shelf adorned with an array of hardware supplies. With an infectious grin, she reached out and seized a gleaming saw, its blade promising the precision and sharpness she required for her daring endeavor.

Armed with her newfound tool, she skipped up to her chained beau, who extended rotten hands in an attempt to grab her. In her state of thinking, she mistook his advancements as an offering of affection. There was a profound tenderness in her gaze as she neared him, her mind fixed on her goal.

With a deep breath and a steady hand, she set to work, the metallic rasp of the handsaw filling the air as she meticulously severed Zed's decaying arms. It was a gruesome sight, to be sure, but she remained resolute, her focus unwavering as she sliced through sinew and bone with steadfast precision.

With a sickening dull sound, the final arm fell to the ground, causing her to withdraw and her chest to heave from the combination of physical strain and excitement. She cast a glance at Zed, now disarmed (quite literally), and experienced a strange sense of satisfaction wash over her.

Convinced that her undead lover could no longer pose a threat to her safety, she began her training regimen in earnest. With patience and perseverance, she taught him to respond to simple commands, rewarding his clumsy attempts with a pat on the head or a murmured word of praise. What she wanted more than anything was affection.

She went to great lengths to show her devotion, indulging in increasingly bizarre acts of attachment. She ventured out into the abandoned streets, scavenging for pieces of dead humans to feed him, relishing the outrageous display as he hungrily devoured the offerings. At each feeding session, she would stroke his decaying back, her fingers probing the pus-filled holes with disturbing infatuation.

In moments of intimacy, she would sit opposite him, gazing lovingly into his expressionless black eyes, oblivious to the fetid stench that emanated from his putrefying form. She would whisper sweet nothings to him, professing her undying love in a voice tinged with madness and desperation.

Joanne's obsession with Zed knew no bounds. During periods of deranged bonding, she would pick up one of his lopped-off arms and hold his decayed hand, intertwining her fingers with his skeletal digits. Yet even during these morbid displays of affection, she found herself yearning for more.

Driven by an insatiable desire for connection, her actions grew ever more erratic and unsettling. She would spend hours talking to him, pouring out her deepest secrets and desires to his unresponsive form, as if seeking validation from a creature incapable of understanding or reciprocating her emotions.

In her neediness for attention, she would sometimes resort to even more extreme measures. She would press her cheek against his cold, decaying flesh, reveling in the gross sensation as she whispered words of passion and devotion into his ear, her voice filled with longing and insanity.

But no matter how much she poured her heart and soul into their warped relationship, Zed only did what zombies do—groan, moan, and snap his jaws in hunger. And yet, despite the ineffectiveness of her efforts, she refused to give up on her undead lover, clinging to the hope that one day, he would return her affections in kind.

As the weeks passed, Joanne's yearning for love only grew stronger, overshadowing any rational thoughts of the risks involved. Fueled by reckless willpower and urgency, she found herself leaning in towards him, her heart pounding with desire as she puckered up for what she believed would be a passionate encounter.

But as their lips met, her romantic moment turned into a nightmare. The sharp pain of Zed's rotten teeth sinking into her flesh shattered the illusion of passion, leaving her horrified and disgusted as she pulled away, blood trickling from her wounded mouth.

Salty liquid welled up in her eyes as she stared at him, her dream of a zombie romance crushed by the harsh reality of her situation. But then, amidst her despair, a spark of lunacy flickered in her eyes as an idea took hold of her mind.

Wiping away her tears, she leaned in for a second smooch. This time, she welcomed his bite, allowing him to gnaw into her flesh with a reckless abandon born of hunger.

She closed her eyes and waited, her heart racing with a deep longing. This was her chance, her opportunity to be with him forever, even if it meant sacrificing her humanity in the process.

Excited and ready, she unchained him, her body fluttering with eagerness for the inevitable transformation. But as the moments passed and nothing happened, a sense of panic began to rise within her.

But then, just as despair threatened to consume her, she sensed a strange radiance wash over her, a tingling spreading from the wound on her mouth to every corner of her being. With a gasp of wonder, she viewed in awe as her skin started to pale, her eyes clouding over with a milky haze as the transmutation took hold.

As the last vestiges of her humanity slipped away, Joanne threw herself into Zed's waiting, limbless arms, her unbeating heart overflowing with a new kind of passion, hunger.

Zombie Poems: 6

A zombie-themed funeral, an odd affair,
Forget mourning, let's lighten the air.
No solemn tears, just laughter and jest,
"Zombies, bid farewell!" my undead rest.

***

Juggling chainsaws with a mischievous grin,
Forget safety, let the chaos begin.
No cautionary tales, just a risky spree,
"Zombies, catch my act!" my danger decree.

***

Neon camouflage for a zombie stroll,
Forget blending in, let's brighten the goal.
No subtlety here, just vibrant hues,
"Zombies, see me now!" my colorful ruse.

***

A zombie-themed lottery, a game of fate,
Forget survival plans, let's gamble and wait.
No careful strategies, just tickets to sell,
"Zombies, try your luck!" my lottery shell.

Chapter 45

In the heart of the city, where concrete jungles met their organic counterparts, a lone figure darted across the rooftops with unparalleled agility. Max, the self-proclaimed Parkour King in a world overrun by the undead, moved with a grace and speed that defied the chaos below.

His belief in his abilities was unwavering, his confidence unshakeable, even in the face of thousands of hungry zombies. In the desolate streets, he prowled like a predator, his senses attuned to the slightest movement. His stomach growled with hunger, a constant reminder of the scarcity of food in this forsaken place. Veering down an alley in search of sustenance, Max's path was halted by a horrifying sight.

A group of the undead, their rotting forms illuminated by the faint glow of the moon, shambled toward him with a relentless appetite. His instinct screamed at him to flee, to retreat back the way he came. But something stirred within him, a reckless defiance that dared him to challenge the encroaching horde. Without hesitation, he launched himself toward the nearest concrete wall, his muscles coiling with a primal energy as he vaulted over the obstacle. For a fleeting moment, he believed he was safe, his heart pounding with a rush of excitement as he landed on the other side.

All at once, a sickening thud drew his attention. He gazed in disbelief at the decaying forms falling over the barrier, their gnarled limbs tangled in a deformed eagerness to get at him. Panic surged through Max's veins as he realized the revenants had found a way to follow him. With a need to see how, he leapt onto the boundary and stared in horror. They were using each other to climb on top of one another to get to the other side.

Shaking off the realization that the zombies were exhibiting intelligence, he felt a gleam in his eyes as he took off, his feet pounding against the cracked asphalt as he sprinted away. Behind him, the horde of hungry deadheads stumbled in pursuit, their deep cries echoing through the empty streets.

He approached a towering building, his heart racing with exhilaration. With a burst of speed, he leaped towards the obstacle, his fingers finding purchase on the crumbling bricks as he began to scale the sheer surface. Each movement was calculated, every foothold carefully chosen as he ascended higher.

Like a spider ascending its web, Max moved with fluidity and precision, his body defying gravity as he climbed to the heavens. The wind whipped past him, carrying the faint scent of decay as he reached the halfway point of his ascent.

With a final burst of effort, he propelled himself upward, his muscles straining against the pull of downward force as he dragged himself onto the rooftop. As he stood atop the high rise structure, a proud grin spread across his face, his ego swelling with pride.

Perched on the edge, Max surveyed the scene below with disdain. The zombies clawed and gnashed at the space below, their hunger-fueled frenzy taking on a whole new perspective. He watched them scramble on top of each other. For a while, he thought they would reach him, but with a sigh of relief, he saw that they lacked the numbers to achieve the height of the building.

With a contemptuous sneer, he leaned forward, his legs dangling over the rim as he spat down at the horde. The glob of saliva arced through the air, landing with a sickening squelch over the decaying skulls of the writhing mass of undead flesh. A chorus of enraged growls rose up from the infected, but he remained unflinching, his arrogance unshakeable as he taunted the creatures.

With a cocky smirk, he turned away from the ledge, surveying which way to go. His face lit up when he realized he could jump from that rooftop to the adjacent one. For him, the world was his playground, and the rotters were nothing more than obstacles to be overcome.

Max's movements were a glide of precision and grace as he leaped effortlessly from one building to the next, scaled walls with the finesse of a spider and flipped over barriers as if defying gravity itself. His antics drew the attention of another group of rotting corpses below, who groaned and stumbled in futile attempts to catch him.

He soared from one rooftop to another, executing a flawless somersault mid-air. He landed with a thud right in the path of an unexpected obstacle—a crude barricade made of mismatched mattresses. With a grunt of surprise, he tumbled over the soft barrier, his fall cushioned by the padding.

Emerging from behind the beds was an old man wielding a cane as a weapon, his eyes wide with terror as he mistook him for one of the undead.

"Back, foul creature!" the old man shouted, waving his walking stick in a wild arc.

"Whoa, easy there, grandpa!" he called out, scrambling to his feet and dodging the swinging rod with a nimble leap. "I'm not a zombie, I swear! Just a man trying to survive!"

But the old man was not convinced. His dedication was matched only by his lack of agility. With a wheeze and a hobble, he pursued Max across the roof, his cries echoing in the night air. Max managed to outmaneuver his geriatric adversary, leaving the old man huffing and puffing as he disappeared into the urban landscape.

But as he bounded away, disaster struck. In a moment of overconfidence, he leaped over a ledge and landed in the middle of a pack of hungry zombies. With a sickening crunch, his right ankle gave way, and pain shot through his left wrist as he tried to break his fall.

Grimacing through the discomfort, he attempted to push himself up, but his busted body refused to obey. Panic set in as he realized he could no longer rely on his Parkour prowess to escape. Frantically scanning his surroundings for an exit route, his eyes settled on a nearby dumpster.

Summoning every ounce of strength, he dragged himself towards the bin, his movements hampered by the excruciating agony radiating from his injuries. With trembling hands, he grasped the lid and began to lift it, only to be greeted by a chorus of screeching raccoons bursting out from within.

Startled and bewildered, he stumbled backward, his heart pounding in his chest. In his moment of hesitation, the zombies closed in, their rotting fingers reaching out to ensnare him in their grasp. With no ability to use his busted limbs, he could only stare helplessly as the horde descended upon him.

The stench of decay mingled with the metallic tang of blood as the undead drew nearer, their hunger-driven groans echoing around him. Max's thoughts raced, searching for a way out, but all he found was the looming inevitability of his demise.

Zombie Music Trivia: Round 7

1. Which Swedish metal band released the song "Zombie Inc." in 2004?
2. What is the name of the American rock band known for their song "Zombie Stomp"?
3. Which British rock band released the song "Zombie Love" in 2009?
4. What is the name of the American punk band known for their song "Zombie Girlfriend"?
5. Which American heavy metal band released the song "Zombie Blood Nightmare" in 2009?
6. What is the name of the American rock band known for their song "Zombie Killer"?

Answers on next page.

1. In Flames
2. Saliva
3. Bad Wolves
4. The Aquabats
5. Gama Bomb
6. Death by Stereo

Chapter 46

Despair hung heavy in the air as Adam sat in his car. The weight of unemployment had shattered his hopes and dreams. At thirty-two, he never imagined he'd be jobless. Yet here he was, grappling with the harsh reality of his situation. Seeking solace in comfort food, he made his way to the local mall, a familiar retreat in times of distress.

Entering the food court, Adam's senses were assaulted by the tantalizing aroma of sizzling meat and spicy sauces. With a gloomy heart, he ordered a generous portion of deep-fried pork drenched in hot sauce, indulging in a guilty pleasure to momentarily escape his troubles. As if that wasn't enough, he added a decadent cream-filled dessert to his order, seeking satisfaction in the temporary relief found in the gratifying indulgence of a fatty meal.

Sitting alone at a table, Adam ignored the warning signs of his irritable bowel syndrome, a common nuisance he often pushed aside in moments of weakness. With a mixture of defiance and resignation, he devoured his feast, losing himself in the blissful oblivion of dripping fat and oozing textures, forgetting his woes if for but a brief time.

Within minutes of finishing his indulgent spread, the recognizable rumblings of his digestive system escalated into a frantic urgency. Panic rising, he rushed to the nearest restroom, barely making it to a stall before the explosive onset of diarrhea.

As he grappled with his humiliating predicament, the world around him descended into madness. A sudden outbreak of zombies was plunging the mall into bedlam, turning ordinary shoppers into flesh-eating monsters.

Trapped in the confines of his locked stall, he could only listen in horror as the once-familiar sounds of men using the washroom morphed into guttural snarls and animalistic growls. Dread coiled in his stomach as he understood the significance of his situation.

With bated breath, he peered through the narrow gap beneath the door, his heart pounding in his chest at the sight of the undead milling about outside.

Fear gripped him as he contemplated his outcome, wondering if he too would succumb to the same gruesome transformation.

Time crawled at an agonizing snail's pace as he waited in terror. Each passing moment stretched out like an eternity. Yet, to his disbelief, he remained unchanged, spared from the grisly destiny that befell others.

Summoning every ounce of courage, to ensure he wasn't heard he finished without flushing and prepared to leave the safety of his stall. With trembling hands, he unlocked the door, hoping to make a swift and silent escape.

As the bolt clicked and the door swung open, Adam's worst nightmare unfolded before his eyes. A ravenous zombie lurched forward, shoving him back into the confines of the stall with brutal force.

Desperation clawed at him as he struggled to evade the grasp of the undead assailant. In a frantic bid for survival, he clambered onto the rim of the seat, seeking refuge in the adjacent stall.

But the creature was inexorable, its decaying arms reaching out to ensnare him in a monstrous dance of death. In a harrowing struggle, he was overpowered. As the ghoul pulled him back into his stall, Adam stumbled, losing his balance. While he tried to avoid the zombie's decomposing fingers, he lost his footing and his body fell forward.

With the deadhead grabbing at him for purchase, he was unable to regain his stability. Dropping to his knees, his back pressed against the rotting corpse and his head collided with the rim of the toilet. He struggled to get up, but within the tight space, there was no room. The revenant attempted to climb over him to get at his brains. As a result, Adam's head was shoved downward, plunging into the filthy enclosure of the crapper, where he found himself drowning in a sickening stew of his own waste.

In a desperate attempt, Adam lifted his head out of the bowl, gagging and spitting out his own poop, blowing it out of his nose in revulsion. He gasped for breath, his lungs burning with the exertion, and drew in a huge lungful of fetid air.

Then, as he tried to escape the clutches of the zombie, his feet slipped and he slid in his own dung with all the grace of a newborn giraffe on an ice rink. His limbs thrashed beneath him, sending globs of fecal matter splattering across the walls and the toilet in a foul chorus of filth.

With each frantic effort to regain his footing, he covered the surrounding surfaces in a slick layer of excrement. The squelching and sloshing sounds echoed off the partitions and tiles, transforming the once-pristine restroom into a nightmarish scene straight out of Jurassic Park.

The zombie also found itself on the receiving end of Adam's stool-fueled escape attempt, its decaying form now coated in a vile mixture of bodily waste. The wet smatterings of feces on its rotting flesh resembled a repulsive masterpiece painted with excrement.

Along with a squishy sound that echoed through the washroom, the nauseating stench filled the air with an unmistakable odor. Adam was repeatedly dragged down toward the white porcelain bowl, his head plunging into the noxious depths of his own manure. The rancid aroma assaulted his senses, threatening to overwhelm him as he gagged and spluttered, his efforts at evasion hampered by the slippery surface beneath him.

Each time he attempted to hoist his body up, the zombie's endeavors to bite his skull pushed him back down. Adam floundered like a car stuck in a muddy quagmire, every wasted attempt to gain traction sending a cascade of muck in all directions. He fought to find stable ground amidst the treacherous, slick morass.

It was a shocking exhibition, his frantic struggles akin to a desperate swimmer caught in a whirlpool of waste. His flailing movements were punctuated by gruff gurgles and gasps for air, his dignity sinking faster than the Titanic in a sea of toilet water and regret. Then pain shot through his head as the undead corpse sank its teeth into him, tearing flesh from his skull.

As the last traces of his life spluttered away, Adam's world faded into darkness, consumed by the incessant tide of the zombies. And in that final moment of despair, he joined the ranks of the living dead.

Zombie Poems: 7

Neon "Zombie Crossing" signs in the street,
Forget caution, let's be indiscreet.
No careful steps, just signs to display,
"Zombies, cross here!" my wayward array.

***

Lemonade stands in a world gone mad,
Forget hiding, let's make zombies glad.
No quiet sips, just a fruity cheer,
"Zombies, take a sip!" my refreshing frontier.

***

A zombie-themed debate, a verbal brawl,
Forget silence, let opinions sprawl.
No hushed tones, just arguments loud,
"Zombies, weigh in!" my vocal crowd.

***

A zombie-themed book club, an intellectual dive,
Forget quiet reading, let's let ideas thrive.
No silence for me, just discussions and strife,
"Zombies, share your thoughts!" my literary life.

Chapter 47

In a world plunged into chaos by the indefatigable onslaught of the undead, two souls shared a fate that was both intertwined and torn asunder. Conjoined at the head, Addison and Madison navigated the harrowing landscape of the zombie apocalypse, their destinies entangled yet divergent.

At the dawn of the outbreak, the sisters had agreed to listen to each other, their bond forged through years of joint experiences and struggles. But as days stretched into weeks and survival became an ever more elusive dream, their unity began to fracture under the weight of their disparate desires.

"We need to head underground, Maddy. It's the safest option."

"But Addy, I don't want to be stuck in a dark, cramped space! I'd rather take our chances on a boat."

"A ship? Madison are you serious? We'd be sitting ducks out on the water!"

"Oh, come on Addison, be realistic. I'd prefer to try our luck at sea over being buried alive below the surface!"

Their disagreements erupted into heated arguments. Each sister was as stubborn as the other as they clung to their own visions of salvation. They clashed like opposing forces of nature, their conflicting wills sending them careening in opposite directions.

Addy would stride forward with determination, only to be jerked back as Maddy attempted to veer off-course. The resulting rebound effect left them slamming into one another, leaving them both bewildered and their movements uncoordinated.

The conjoining of their forms hindered their progress, rendering them slow and ungainly. Forced to walk in a perpetual sideways shuffle, they resembled sidestepping crabs traversing a treacherous shore. It wasn't just their brains that determined their outcome, it was the physical burden of their shared body that weighed them down.

Under the dim glow of the moonlight, they engaged in a heated argument, their voices rising with tension as they grappled with their emotions. Their loud exchange caught the attention of a single zombie lurking nearby. Drawn by the disturbance, the undead creature staggered toward the sisters with hungry desire.

When it closed in, they reacted fast, their conjoined bodies twisting and contorting to fend off the approaching threat. In the frantic struggle, the deadhead managed to sink its teeth into Addison's arm, tearing through her flesh with a sickening crunch. Addison cried out in agony, her screams filling the streets as she clutched her wounded limb.

The sudden outburst of noise caught the attention of a lone survivor, who had been navigating the deserted city in search of food. Sensing trouble, he hurried toward the source of the disturbance, his hand gripping the his trusty firearm. With practiced precision, he took aim and fired a fatal shot at the zombie, its decaying head exploding in a burst of gore as it crumpled to the ground.

The girls watched in shock, their eyes wide with disbelief at the sudden turn of events. Before they could react, the man vanished into the darkness without a word, leaving them alone once again in the silent night.

With quivering limbs, the sisters struggled to their feet, their conjoined bodies moving in an awkward shuffle as they put distance between themselves and the scene of the encounter. Fear and confusion gripped their hearts while they stumbled through the streets, their minds racing with the implications of what had just transpired.

As they searched for a safe refuge, Addison's condition began to deteriorate, the telltale signs of disease spreading through her wounded arm. Maddy watched in horror as her sister's skin took on a sickly ashen hue and her movements became sluggish and clumsy. Tears welled in her eyes as she recognized the grim truth—Addison was turning into one of the zombies.

With a heavy heart, Madison came to terms with the devastating reality of their situation. She knew that there was no way to save her sister, no cure for the infection that was consuming her from within. In a moment of profound sadness, she made a solemn vow to herself—she would do whatever it took to protect her sibling, even if it meant dragging her lifeless body along with her as they navigated the dangerous world of the undead.

With deformed vividness, the change was complete. Addison's head, now possessed by the insatiable appetite of the rotters, constantly snapped and gnashed at the air, her teeth gnashing at Madison's body. Trapped in an unholy union, the sisters were forever bound by the distorted destiny that had befallen them.

In a moment of anguish, Madison realized there was no escape from the grisly fate that awaited them. With resignation, she dragged her twin into an oncoming pack of the infected, bracing herself for the inevitable bite that never came. To her disbelief, the other zombies regarded them with an eerie sense of recognition, as if they were one of their own. In a roundabout way, Maddy found she was stuck between both worlds, neither fully alive nor truly dead.

As Addison, now a full-fledged zombie, chomped down on a hapless survivor cornered by the undead horde, Madison could only stare in shock. She tried desperately to pry her sister away from the dying human, but Addison's insatiable hunger knew no bounds. Each attempt to intervene brought about unsuccessful struggles. Their conjoined bodies snapped back together like elastic bands, fused like their heads. This resulted in a contorted, agonizing tangle of limbs as they writhed in a forced embrace.

As days turned into weeks, Madison attempted to adjust to her new reality, but the weight of her loss pressed heavily upon her. The absence of her twin, her closest companion, left a gaping void in her heart that seemed impossible to fill. Every passing moment was a reminder of the bond they once shared, now severed by the cruel hand of fate.

Driven by despair and an urgent longing to be reunited with her sister, Madison made the agonizing decision to join Addison in undeath. With a deep inhale and a whooshing exhale, she summoned her courage, dragging her arm upward and thrusting it towards Addy's mouth. But she did not respond, her sister's undead state rendering her unresponsive to Madison's desperate attempts.

"Why won't you bite me?" she howled. Frustration overwhelmed Maddy as she sank to the ground, towing Addy with her. Her eyes fell on the pavement scattered with debris. Amidst the rubble, she spotted a plastic bag, a simple last-ditch solution forming in her mind.

With shaky hands, she draped the sack over her twin's head, tearing a hole in it to accommodate their conjoined form. Rising to her feet, she pulled Addison along as they ventured into a group of zombies.

The irregular movements caused by their attached state threatened to send her tumbling, but she fought to maintain her balance, determined to carry out her plan. At first, the other creatures paid little attention to her presence, their vacant stares betraying no recognition of the breathing soul among them.

Undeterred, she persisted, throwing her arms out in a bid to provoke a reaction. Finally, one of the rotters took notice, lurching forward with hungry anticipation. Relief washed over her as she embraced her new identity, knowing she would never be alone in this world of the living and the dead.

Zombie Music Trivia: Round 8

1. Which Irish rock band released the song "Zombie Man" in 2013?
2. What is the name of the American metal band known for their song "Zombie Slam"?
3. Which American punk band released the song "Zombie World" in 1983?
4. What is the name of the American rock band known for their song "Zombie Riot"?
5. Which Finnish symphonic metal band released the song "Zombie Slam" in 2008?
6. What is the name of the American rock band known for their song "Zombie Prostitute"?

Answers on next page.

1. Flogging Molly
2. Pain
3. The Misfits
4. Alien Ant Farm
5. Lordi
6. Voltaire

Chapter 48

The relentless beat of rain hitting the windshield masked the sound of her pounding heart as she huddled in the driver's seat of the battered sedan. Tina's twitching hands gripped the steering wheel, her knuckles white against the cold metal. How had it come to this?

It had started as a routine drive through the countryside, the rhythm of the road lulling her into a false sense of security. The storm had rolled in with a vengeance, reducing visibility to near zero. Lightning cracked the sky, illuminating the hazardous path ahead. In a split-second decision, Tina had swerved to avoid a fallen tree, her tires skidding on the slick roadway.

The car careened off the road, crashing through a flimsy barrier and hurtling into the gloom below. The sickening sensation of weightlessness seized her as the vehicle plummeted, landing with a bone-jarring crash at the bottom of the quarry.

The rain poured persistently, obscuring Tina's view through the windshield of the sedan as she sat trapped at the deepest part of the pit. Panic gripped her as she glimpsed through the back windows and mirrors to witness an excessively large group of zombies emerging from the darkness. They stumbled toward her like clumsy dancers, their moans echoing off the stone walls. They had followed the uproar of her crashing car, drawn by the promise of fresh meat.

Her pulse thrummed in her ears as she realized the importance of her situation. Surrounded by a sea of undead, she was trapped inside the vehicle, unable to open any of the doors and make a break for it. She fumbled for her cell phone, desperate to call for help, but her hopes were dashed when she discovered there was no cellular coverage. Turning it over in her hand, she dared not use it for anything else with the battery dwindling down fast.

As the night wore on, her anxiety grew. The rain ceased, giving way to an oppressive silence broken only by the distant moans of the zombies. She shivered in the cold, huddled in the back seat with her meager supplies—a half-empty water bottle, a cracked mobile, and a single chocolate bar.

Morning dawned with a cruel intensity, the sun beating down mercilessly on the automobile. The temperature inside the vehicle increased so quickly that it was like being in an oven. She realized she was in trouble.

With no means of escape and limited provisions, she faced the grim reality of her predicament. She was going to cook alive in the motorcar, a fortune as absurd as it was tragic.

As the hours stretched on, Tina's delirium grew. She found herself engaging in one-sided conversations with the zombies outside, fantasizing their grunts and groans as replies to her desperate pleas for help. She even gave them names—Larry, with two missing limbs, and Mildred, with the distinctive limp.

"So, old buddy, playing tennis today? Oh, wait, you can't, you haven't any arms! Sorry about that, didn't mean to rub it in." She chuckled, imagining him shrugging in response, or at least attempting to with his lack of limbs. There was nothing but a stillness from beyond, broken only by the moans of the zombies.

"Young lady, how many humans have you killed?" Tina raised one brow and pictured her pausing and then groaning an exaggerated number. "Did I hear that right? 500 people so far and still counting? Gee, you are a champion at murdering."

More quietness, punctuated by the occasional thud against the car.

"You know, guys, I've been thinking, who were you before? And who are you now?" She tilted her head, imagining them exchanging confused glances, then resuming their mindless pursuit.

"Oh, I see, you're not quite the introspective types. Just deadheads on a mission."

But Tina couldn't resist weaving stories for them in her mind. "Larry, my man, I wouldn't have pictured you as an accountant. Were you the kind who loved spreadsheets, or the one who always nodded off during meetings?" She snickered at the mental image of him, now undead, struggling with Excel.

"And you, Mildred, a brain surgeon? Noteworthy career change! I bet you had steady hands back then. Now, not so much, huh?" She chuckled, imagining her attempting surgery with her rotting clumsiness.

The ghouls outside showed just how uninterested in her questions they were by continuing to shuffle and slam into the vehicle.

"Okay, I get it. You're not the chatty type. But you do groan a lot, Both of you. I'm here, come get me!" she said, pressing her face against the window. She flinched when together they banged into the door, their limbs reaching for her with fingers sliding down the glass.

The interior temperature continued to climb, turning the sedan into a sweltering oven. With each passing minute, the heat intensified, seeping into every crevice of the car and enveloping her in a suffocating embrace. She could feel the sweat pooling at the small of her back, trickling down her spine in an unstoppable stream. The fabric of her garments clung to her skin, soaked through with perspiration as she gasped for air in the stifling heat.

In a desperate bid to cool herself down, she began to peel off her clothing, discarding it with a sense of defeat. Her shirt came off first, followed by her pants, until she was wearing only her undergarments. She sat in the driver's seat, the leather sticking uncomfortably to her damp body.

Glancing around, she saw groups of creatures to her left and right, but ahead lay a clear path to a dump truck. But surrounded by zombies, she understood that escaping without them catching her was impossible. Frustrated, she pondered how to reach the heavy-duty transport. An idea struck—she'd pull down the back seats exit through the trunk, and escape in the darkness of night. But with six hours until sunset, uncertainty loomed.

Trembling, she rolled the window down slightly, hoping for fresh air. Instead, stifling humidity poured in, making the atmosphere unbearable. Climbing into the back, she struggled to drag the seats down. After several attempts, she succeeded, pausing to wipe sweat from her forehead before squeezing into the trunk among bags and a spare tire.

With her body contorted, she reached for the release lever, anticipating her escape. But her hopes were dashed when she discovered that the trunk was caved in from the accident and it wouldn't open. She kicked it, banged on it with fisted hands, and then, with fuming anger, she crawled back to the front seat.

With an audible sigh, she turned to the creatures beside her door and said, "Well, Mildred, Larry, it's been real. But I can't say I'll miss this cozy little carpool we've had going on."

She glanced around at the undead horde surrounding her vehicle, their vacant stares sending a strong shudder across her neck. "Looks like it's just you and me now, folks. Guess it's time for me to make my grand exit."

Her tone shifted to a sarcastic smirk as she continued, "And by 'exit,' I mean a dramatic escape involving explosions and daring aerial stunts! Or maybe just slowly cooking to death in this car. Yeah, that sounds about right."

The creatures gave no response, their unblinking eyes fixed on her like hungry predators. She shook her head ruefully, resigned to her fate. "What, no standing ovation for my magnificent finale? I'll just have to settle for a slow roast instead."

With a wry chuckle, she settled back in her seat, bracing herself for the inevitable.

Zombie Poems: 8

Insist on having a zombie-themed petting zoo,
Forget caution, let's bond with the undead crew.
No fear in my heart, just cuddles and cheer,
"Zombies, feel the love!" my perilous frontier.

***

Develop a taste for zombie cuisine,
Forget normal food, let's dine so obscene.
No concern for safety, just a daring feat,
"Zombies, here's a bite!" my culinary seat.

***

Carry a giant neon arrow pointing to your location,
Forget subtlety, let's guide with dedication.
No quiet escape, just a bold direction,
"Zombies, this way!" my ill-fated selection.

***

Set up a zombie puppet show,
Forget seriousness, let's let puppets glow.
No solemn tone, just laughs and jest,
"Zombies, enjoy the show!" my puppet zest.

Chapter 49

Ivan moved with practiced precision in the bustling kitchen of his restaurant, The Opal Ristorante. At 44 years old, he was a seasoned chef, famous for his culinary expertise. Today, he was in the middle of creating one of his signature dishes—a delectable beef bourguignon that had earned him rave reviews from food critics and diners alike.

The savory aroma of simmering meat and rich red wine filled the air as he chopped onions with efficiency, his focus solely on the task at hand. He was so absorbed in his work that he didn't pay attention to the commotion in the dining section.

It wasn't until one of his sous chefs stumbled into the kitchen, bloodied and pale, that Ivan's concentration was finally drawn away from his cutting board. Horror washed over him as he took in the scene unfolding before him—his staff and his friends being attacked by a group of diners who had turned into zombies.

Without hesitation, Ivan grabbed a nearby knife and hurled it at the nearest zombie, the blade sinking deep into its rotting flesh. He threw another, then six more, but the undead creature continued to advance, unfazed by the knives sticking out of it. Its empty eyes fixed on him with an insatiable hunger.

Panic surged through him as he realized the magnitude of the situation. With his staff overwhelmed and no time to waste, he made a split-second decision. He dashed toward the large freezer at the back of the kitchen, believing it was his only chance at survival.

He slipped inside the freezer, the cold air hitting him like a slap in the face. Recognizing that shutting the door would result in him freezing to death, he utilized a frozen object to prop it open just enough to squeeze through.

Huddled in the corner, he peered out through the narrow opening, watching in horror as a sous chef succumbed to the zombie virus, transforming into one of the undead before his very eyes. The speed of the transformation was staggering, sending chills down Ivan's back as he grasped the scale of the situation.

Time seemed to blur as he waited, his mind racing with thoughts of survival. He understood that he had to keep moving, to find a way out of this nightmare. With grim perseverance, he scanned around for anything he could use as a weapon.

His eyes landed on a frozen leg of lamb, and he snatched it up, preparing himself for the inevitable moment when the zombies would stumble upon him. The minutes ticked by while he grew colder and more furious.

In a dramatic turn of events, the barrier propping the door open was kicked out by a wandering undead, allowing a zombie to amble in. This left Ivan with a spine-tingling sensation as the door then sealed itself shut. "Goddamn it!" he yelled. "Look at what you did, you bloody zombified idiot. Now I'm stuck in here." Using the leg of lamb, he beat the reanimated rotter over the head until it lay motionless on the floor. He checked for any signs of movement, ensuring that the creature was dead.

With no time to waste, he had to find a way out before he froze to death. His gaze landed on a large bovine carcass hanging from a butcher's meat hook, and an idea began to form in his mind. Directly above it was an air vent, which would be his saving grace. Ivan wrapped his arms around the lower part of the animal and attempted to shimmy up its body. But to his dismay, he found himself sliding down, the frozen beef too slippery to gain a proper grip.

Frustration surged through him as he grasped the ineffectiveness of his efforts. He stood beside the massive bovine, a bead of sweat forming on his brow despite the freezing temperature. "Ole girl, you sure are a stubborn bitch," he muttered under his breath.

His gaze swept across the room, searching for an alternative solution. Then, an idea struck him like a bolt of lightning. With a renewed sense of determination, he disappeared into another part of the freezer, returning moments later with two meat hooks in hand.

He didn't waste a second before plunging them into the carcass, using them as leverage to climb up. But as he attempted to ascend, he understood his mistake—the prongs had penetrated the mass, making them impossible to pull out. Struggling against the cold, he tried to free them from their icy prison. Despite his best attempts, he couldn't get them to move from their fixed position.

Ivan knew he had to come up with another plan. His eyes scanned the confines, searching for anything he could use to assist in his escape. Then it dawned on him—the boxes of frozen food stacked on the shelves. With a newfound sense of resolution, he set to work, gathering the cartons and stacking them into a makeshift ladder.

Once it was assembled, he wasted no time in scrambling to the top. He reached for the vent cover and managed to pry it open. Grunting with effort, he squeezed his head through first, like a determined ostrich trying to bury its head in the sand. With a proud grunt, he used his muscles and hands together to wriggle his shoulders into the opening.

As his body twisted in ways he hadn't experienced since his younger days, he couldn't help but regret indulging in excess for the past twenty years. Just as he began to revel in the small victory of making progress, reality came crashing down upon him like an avalanche.

To his disappointment, his success was short-lived when he discovered that his frame wouldn't fit through the narrow passage. Panic set in as he found himself dangling dangerously from the vent, his head and shoulders wedged tightly between the cold steel and the frozen walls of the duct, like Santa trapped in a chimney only much less graceful.

With no escape and his clothes stuck like glue to the icy enclosure, Ivon considered his next move, feeling as miserable as a stranded polar bear on a melting iceberg. With a final attempt, he mustered all his energy and unleashed a forceful kick, relying on gravity for support. Yet, all he achieved was to knock down his makeshift steps.

Left dangling like a forgotten Christmas ornament, he clung to the hope of an electrical outage that would bring relief from his frosty captivity. With each passing minute, he prayed for the power to go out, fantasizing about thawing his way out of his sticky situation, much like a snowman on a sunny day.

A couple of hours slipped by with no sign of an electricity blackout. He shivered, closing his eyes as memories flooded back to when he was just five years old. It was a time etched with fear and embarrassment, stuck on a waterslide, his young frame too large for the narrow confines. His father had been his savior then, a reassuring presence amidst the chaos. Yet now, as he faced this frozen abyss, there was no one to rescue him, only the bitterness of regret lingering in the icy air.

Zombie Music Trivia: Round 9

1. Which British rock band released the song "Zombie Dance" in 2010?
2. What is the name of the American metal band known for their song "Zombie Messiah"?
3. Which American rock band released the song "Zombie Eaters" in 1989?
4. What is the name of the American rock band known for their song "Zombie Radio"?
5. Which American punk band released the song "Zombie Slide" in 2002?
6. What is the name of the American metal band known for their song "Zombie Dance"?

Answers on next page.

1. The Blackout
2. Six Feet Under
3. Faith No More
4. Gwar
5. Dr. Steel
6. Escape the Fate

Chapter 50

Sally had always prided herself on her resourcefulness. Growing up in a small town, she learned early on how to make do with what she had. But nothing could have prepared her for the chaos that ensued during the zombie apocalypse.

She raced down the hallway of the 15th floor in the thirty-story apartment complex, fear gripping her chest with an iron hold. Desperate for refuge, she pounded on doors, pleading for someone, anyone, to let her in. But each door remained closed, the racket of her pounding fists blending with the moans of the approaching horde.

As she ran blindly, her foot collided with a dead man and she stumbled forward, crashing to the ground with a jolt. Holding back vomit, she gasped at the remains, taking in his injuries and the spilled blood. Dismissing it as best she could, she scrambled to her feet, her body trembling as she tried to steady herself.

But before she could regain her bearings, a decomposing hand shot out from behind her, seizing hold of her shirt with a vise-like grip. With a strangled cry, she heard the fabric tear as she wrenched free, her heart racing as she fled. The chilling touch of death lingered over her skin as she raced for safety.

Hot on her heels, the ravenous zombies were gaining on her, their deep growls mixing with the thundering of their footsteps. With quick thinking, she lunged for the fire hose reel, unfurling it in a swift motion and looping it over door knobs, hoping to trip them up and buy herself some precious time. For a moment, it worked. The undead stumbled, disoriented by the unexpected obstacle, giving Sally a brief reprieve.

But their hunger drove them forward with heightened ferocity, and they soon regained their footing. Their booming steps and haunting grunts pulsating through the corridor as she dashed for the stairwell leading to the rooftop. With each step, the noise grew louder, the unstoppable pursuit of the deadheads creating a chilling backdrop to her frantic exodus.

"Help! Please, someone help!" she cried out. Her voice was lost in a void of nothingness, but her will to survive was unwavering as she raced up the stairs. The hungry droning of the zombies stabbed her ears, a frightening warning of a perilous race against time and death.

She reached the roof of the high-rise building via the emergency exit. Though she had expected to find a fire escape that she could use, all she found was rusty broken steps with no possible way of descending. Her muscles pulled tauter with every distant groan of the undead. The complex was swarming with zombies, and her only chance of survival was getting to the ground below.

She went back to the door, opening it only to discover ambling ghouls now filling the staircase. Closing the door, she walked to the edge of the rooftop and peered over. To her left, more buildings, to her right, a lake. "If only I had wings," she grumbled while taking in the sights around her.

The scent of burning plastic slapped her in the face. She turned to face the other way and saw a neighboring building on fire. For a split second, she worried that it would jump from that structure to where she was. Shaking off the thought, she sat down, contemplating.

Her gaze fixated on a stack of boxes in a corner, and her curiosity got the better of her. She got up and headed for it, pulling the cardboard aside and brushing cobwebs and dust into the air. Beneath, she discovered a pile of old bedsheets.

She tossed them out of the way and took herself to the opposite side of the rooftop. Her thoughts on how to get down grew more urgent when the sounds of slamming, banging, and thudding reached her ears.

She looked toward the door. Though it was reinforced steel, she believed they would beat it down. Then her eyes went back to the heap of sheets she had found, and an idea struck her. "I've got it!" she cried, rushing off to where they were.

Without hesitation, she grabbed them and began to fashion them into an improvised parachute. She remembered seeing something similar in a movie once and hoped that her memory served her well.

Her heart fluttered as she tied the knots, her fingers fumbling with the fabric. She could feel the weight of the impending danger bearing down on her as she worked, the urgency of the situation fueling her grit.

After some time, Sally stepped back to admire her handiwork. The chute was far from perfect, but it would have to do. With a deep breath, she hoisted the contraption onto her back and raced around the rooftop to gauge if it would work. Devoid of wind, she couldn't figure out if it would or not, until a heavy pounding on the door got her moving. "It's now or never," she said, moving to the ledge.

She stood on the rim, peering down at the ground below. Doubt crept into her mind. What if it failed? What if she ended up plummeting to her death instead of making a daring escape?

But there was no time for second-guessing. The zombies were closing in, their hungry moans growing louder with each passing moment. With a silent prayer on her lips, she walked back twenty feet, and then took a running start and launched herself off the roof of the building.

For a while, time seemed to stand still as Sally fell through the air. The wind whipped past her face, and the ground rushed up to meet her with frightening speed. But just as panic began to grip her, she spread her arms and let the sheets open up, bracing for the jerk of the parachute deploying.

Except it didn't.

Instead of billowing out and slowing her descent, the bedsheets remained wrapped around her body, offering no resistance to the force of gravity. She screamed in terror as she hurtled towards the concrete, the impact looming ever closer with each passing second.

In a mad effort, she tried to untangle the linens, but it was no use. The ground was mere moments away now, and there was nothing she could do to stop her inevitable fate.

With a sickening bang, she crashed onto the pavement below. The collision knocked the breath from her lungs and sent searing pain shooting through her body. Shocked that the fall didn't kill her, she realized that her back, legs, and neck were nonetheless shattered despite her padding. Death would come anyway, she told herself.

As darkness closed in around her, she could hear the faraway sounds of the zombies drawing near, their hungry snarls signaling the end of her journey.

Zombie Music Trivia: Round 10

1. Which American rock band released the song "Zombie Dance" in 1980?
2. Which song by Rob Zombie features lyrics about a mysterious figure who drives a hot rod named "Dragula"?
3. Which American punk band released the song "Zombie Movie" in 2003?
4. What is the name of the American rock band known for their song "Zombie Onslaught"?
5. Which Australian metalcore band released the song "Zombie Autopilot" in 2004?
6. What is the name of the American rock band known for their song "Zombie Night"?

Answers on next page.

1. The Cramps
2. Dragula
3. The Meteors
4. Municipal Waste
5. Parkway Drive
6. Wednesday 13

Chapter 51

As I sit here reflecting on the events of the recent past and dictating my thoughts onto my digital recorder, a smirk plays on the edges of my lips. What a bunch of dumbasses those people were in all those stories! And they're just the ones I know of so far, the tip of the iceberg. I'm sure I'll uncover many more such losers all around the world as time goes on, since—let's face it—most of us hairless apes simply aren't all that bright.

How did I learn how these people met their demise, you may ask? Largely from security camera footage and smartphones where such devices were active, and via word-of-mouth in other cases. You see, future anthropologist, I'm a computer hacker. And the Internet is still up so far, and there's still power, so I've been able to peruse such data in my leisure time—which I have an ample amount of these days, when I'm not hunting and foraging.

And why am I recording these humorous tales of woe, you may also ask? Well, I figure scholarly human survivors of this plague will most likely eventually create dry, nonfictional accounts of the events from historical and scientific perspectives. So since those niches will be covered, I decided to record for posterity just how dumb people can be in this kind of situation—you know, for 'shits and giggles' or whatever. Of course, I had to dramatize the stories somewhat and invent some conversations based on the facts—but I think it's important that someone record the humor and pathos inherent even in the face of catastrophic disaster, black as it may be at times. And I'm just the guy for the job.

Come on, you have to admit, these people were funny! They were so blind, so naïve—and so unlike me. Oh, how they stumbled through their lives—and then their deaths—lacking imagination and blissfully unaware of the dangers lurking around every corner, with no idea of how to cope with the unthinkable when it happened for real. But not me! I was always one step ahead, my intellect guiding me through the chaos unscathed. I survived! And I will continue to do so, thanks to my foresight and my meticulous preparations.

But wait... Now the hairs on the back of my neck are standing on end as a faint noise reverberates in the distance, growing louder with each passing moment. Could it be... Yes, it's a ferryboat. And it's headed straight for my private island! I raise my binoculars for a closer look, and my chest is tightening as I see who the occupants of that boat are.

Both the upper and lower decks of the ferry are jam-packed with repulsive-looking zombies, wall-to-wall. But who is piloting the boat? Maybe one or more of the disgusting creatures developed or retained some semblance of intelligence—which is something I hadn't counted on. But that would be breaking the zombie rules! Or is it just dumb luck? Did they infest a boat that was already underway and it went off-course? That's probably a more likely explanation. But in any case, it appears I'm to finally come face-to-face with the horror I thought I'd eluded forever. No fair, I say!

They're getting close enough now that I can hear their incessant moaning. Where can I go? There'll be no hiding from them when they overrun this little island. I have weapons, but I'm only one man and there are so many of them. I guess I'll have to leave this island.

I grab my AR-15, my computer, and my go-bag—See? Always prepared!—and go down to the dock. Now I'll fire up my boat's engine and head out into the bay. I have extra ammo and enough food, water, and fuel to last me a few days, so I should be able to easily reach another island. Off we go...

Huh! What the hell... Now what? I've run aground! But I know I'm not near the reef yet. The sandy shoals must have shifted during a storm. It's been so long since I've had to think about it, that I—well, I didn't think about it. I cut the engine so it won't burn out. It should be shallow enough on the shoal for me to stand and push or pull the boat off it.

Ah, but wait a minute—now there's water coming into the bottom of the boat. Damn! There's a hole in the hull, a sizable one. Is there a patch reef in this spot after all, or did I scrape a rock? I should have surveyed this bay better. And guess what, I don't have anything at hand to repair the hole with. Who would have thought? This boat was supposed to be damn near indestructible and unsinkable, according to the salesman. That fucker!

Well, I can't stay here. Not only will the boat soon fill with water—I see there's another storm about to roll in, and I know the water gets rough when that happens. I'm sure I can swim back to shore from here if I go now, but then what? Well, I'll have to cross that bridge when I come to it.

I wonder if my gun will still work if it gets wet? It's supposed to. Guess I'll find out. I sling it over my shoulder, stick a couple extra magazines in my pockets, and get into the water. I'll have to leave my computer and go-bag behind for now, since they'd be too heavy to swim with. But I do have a plastic bag that my recorder will fit in, so maybe that'll be okay at least. I have to record whatever happens—it's my main purpose in life these days.

Now I'm discovering that jellyfish are washing in with the tide. Is it one of those periodic jelly infestations—another thing I should have paid more attention to—or are they simply being driven in by the storm? Either way, they're stinging me as I swim—and it hurts! But at least they're not Man O' Wars. So there might be some pain and itching for a while, but I shouldn't die from them. Anyway, better start stroking...

Well, I've reached the shore. There's no point in staying in the water, even if I could find a spot with no jellyfish, because the saltwater isn't soothing my stings. Now I guess I'll have to find someplace where I can hide. The storm is darkening the sky and the sun's going down, so maybe the encroaching dark of night will help me. But the dusky fog that's now surrounding me is also making it hard for me to see—and as if to underscore that problem, I just stepped on a jellyfish! I forgot to look down. Christ, now I can see they're all over the beach, and I neglected to put my boat shoes on before I left.

But I have a bigger problem now. Glancing up the beach, I see them—and they see me. A horde of disembarked living dead, their decaying forms emerging from the shadows... They are apparently being drawn to me. Did they see me or smell me? Doesn't much matter, I guess. Man, it's like the beach has birthed a civilization of the undead! There must be at least a couple hundred of the lifeless abominations, all shuffling about like serpents snaking out of the dunes.

I'm trying not to panic. I unsling my rifle and start shooting. The gun still works, but my aim isn't that good because it's hard to see, plus my feet keep getting stung as I walk along the beach. So I'm not scoring headshots, and I know that's the only way to stop them. If I could just make it to those trees... But I think the multiple jellyfish stings must be taking a toll, because I'm finding it hard to move my feet. My whole body hurts and itches all over, and my legs feel like lead pipes.

The loose sand is also proving treacherous, impeding my progress with each faltering step I manage. Ow! I just stumbled and fell, and I think I shot myself in the foot! It's hard to tell because both of my feet are numb now. But yeah, there's blood. Oh, for Pete's sake, I just realized I'm lying in a pile of jellyfish! And now the moans of the undead are getting closer.

What a clusterfuck! How could this have happened to me, of all people? I was tough! I was smart! I was prepared! Well touché, cruel Fate, touché. I laughed at all those dummies, and now I guess I'm getting my comeuppance. I'm about to become yet another dumb example of how NOT to survive a zombie apocalypse.

They're almost upon me now. And I've fallen and I can't get up, ha-ha! I could try to shoot some of them, but why bother? They'll get me in the end. So I guess I'll just put the gun to my own head. At least that way, I won't have to watch them eat me and endure that particular agony, and maybe I won't end up becoming one of them.

Goodbye!

Silly & Dumb Zombie Jokes

1. Why did the zombie go to school?

- *Punchline:* To improve his "dead"-ucation!

2. What's a zombie's favorite cereal?

- *Punchline:* Rotten Bran!

3. Why don't zombies use social media?

- *Punchline:* They've lost their "app"-etite!

4. How do zombies exercise their brains?

- *Punchline:* With "dead" lifts!

5. Why did the zombie bring a ladder to the bar?

- *Punchline:* He heard the drinks were on the house!

6. What do you call a zombie who cooks?

- *Punchline:* A "dead" chef!

7. How does a zombie propose?

- *Punchline:* With a "corpse"-age ring!

8. What's a zombie's favorite dance?

- *Punchline:* The "Thriller Shuffle"!

9. Why did the zombie break up with his girlfriend?

- *Punchline:* She just wasn't his "deady"!

10. What's a zombie's favorite comedy show?

- *Punchline:* "The Walking Deadpan"!

11. What did the zombie say to the bartender?

- *Punchline:* "I'll have a bloody Mary, extra bloody!"

12. How do zombies settle arguments?

- *Punchline:* They have a "dead"lock!

13. Why did the zombie apply for a job at the bakery?

- *Punchline:* He heard they kneaded someone with "bread" experience!

14. What's a zombie's favorite fruit?

- *Punchline:* A "brain"-ana!

15. What do you call a group of musical zombies?

- *Punchline:* The "Undead Symphony"!

16. Why did the zombie start a band?

- *Punchline:* He wanted to "rock" the afterlife!

17. How do zombies keep their hair in place?

- *Punchline:* With "dead" hairspray!

18. What did one zombie say to the other at the party?

- *Punchline:* "You're a real dead-ringer for someone I used to know!"

19. Why did the zombie refuse to play hide and seek?

- *Punchline:* He was tired of "losing his head" over it!

20. How do zombies travel?

- *Punchline:* On the "dead"-icated express!

Intentionally Bad "Survival Tips Gone Wrong"

- Attempt to negotiate with zombies by offering them expired cans of food as a peace offering.
- Decorate your hideout with neon signs flashing "Fresh Brains Here" to attract zombies for a party.
- Taunt zombies by challenging them to a game of zombie tag, thinking they'll enjoy the chase.
- Use a bicycle bell to alert zombies of your presence and engage them in a friendly conversation.
- Carry a boombox playing country music loudly to calm the nerves of nearby zombies.
- Paint yourself with glow-in-the-dark paint to blend in with the zombies during nighttime.
- Wear a shirt with a target painted on it to challenge zombies to a game of "pin the brain on the human."
- Organize a zombie-themed cooking competition and judge their culinary creations made from canned goods and rotten produce.
- Offer zombies a selection of flavored brains to satisfy their cravings, like barbecue or teriyaki.
- Set up a zombie beauty pageant and crown the "Miss Zombie Apocalypse" based on decay and demeanor.
- Attempt to negotiate a truce with zombies by offering them peace treaties written in crayon.
- Organize a zombie Olympics with events like "Undead Limbo" and "Brain Toss."
- Try to teach zombies to play musical instruments and form a zombie band.
- Organize a zombie beach day and provide sandcastle-building supplies for them to enjoy.
- Try to train a group of zombies to perform synchronized swimming routines in a makeshift pool.
- Offer zombies lessons in basic first aid to help them tend to their

wounds and injuries.

- Try to educate zombies on the importance of dental hygiene by offering them undead toothbrushes and floss.
- Organize a zombie support group where they can share their struggles and feelings about being undead.
- Carry a sign saying "Zombie Storytelling Circle" and encourage them to share their memories from before they turned.
- Offer zombies lessons in basic hygiene and sanitation to prevent the spread of disease among their ranks.

- Attempt to distract zombies by performing magic tricks with everyday objects.
- Try to convince zombies to participate in a synchronized dance routine to the tune of "Thriller."
- Train a group of zombies to perform circus acts like tightrope walking and juggling.
- Carry a sign saying "Zombie Karaoke Night" and encourage them to sing their favorite undead anthems.
- Attempt to teach zombies the art of origami to keep their hands and minds occupied.
- Offer zombies lessons in etiquette and manners to improve their social skills.
- Try to teach zombies basic sign language to facilitate communication with the living.
- Offer zombies guided meditation sessions to help them find moments of calm in the midst of chaos.
- Carry a sign saying "Zombie Friendship Circle" and attempt to foster camaraderie and mutual support among them.
- Try to train a group of zombies to perform synchronized swimming routines in a makeshift pool.
- Offer zombies lessons in basic self-defense techniques to help them protect themselves from hostile survivors.
- Carry a sign saying "Zombie Improv Night" and encourage them to participate in spontaneous acting exercises.
- Try to teach zombies basic computer skills to help them navigate the

digital world.

- Offer zombies lessons in environmental conservation and sustainable living practices to help them minimize their impact on the world around them.
- Carry a sign saying "Zombie Game Night" and attempt to engage them in friendly competitions and challenges.
- Try to teach zombies basic sewing and mending skills to help them repair their clothing and gear.
- Offer zombies lessons in conflict resolution and mediation to help them resolve disputes peacefully.
- Carry a sign saying "Zombie Karaoke Extravaganza" and attempt to get them singing along to their favorite songs.
- Try to teach zombies basic woodworking skills to help them construct shelters and furniture.
- Offer zombies lessons in financial literacy and money management to help them navigate the post-apocalyptic economy.

Zombie Movie Quotes

1. White Zombie (1932)

- "I kissed her as she lay there in the coffin." - Legendre (Bela Lugosi)

2. Poultrygeist: Night of the Chicken Dead (2006)

- "What, you didn't see that coming?" - Hummus (Caleb Emerson)

3. Shock Waves (1977)

- "You are like a butcher, and this is the slaughterhouse." - SS Commander (Peter Cushing)

4. The Dead Next Door (1989)

- "Zombies aren't afraid of other zombies." - Raimi (Peter Ferry)

5. World War Z (2013)

- "Movement is life." - Gerry Lane (Brad Pitt)

6. Tombs of the Blind Dead (1972)

- "They are all dead. They just don't know it yet." - The Knight Templar (Fernando Sancho)

7. Aaah! Zombies!, aka Wasting Away (2007)

- "I think we might be dead." - Mike (Michael Grant Terry)

8. Zeder (1983)

- "There's no danger. The dead are very weak." - Stroscio (Cesare Barbetti)

9. Deadgirl (2008)

- "We're talking about the undead here. Do you think they care?" - J.T. (Noah Segan)

10. Warm Bodies (2013)

- "I can't feel my penis." - R (Nicholas Hoult)

11. Little Monsters (2019)

- "That's my signature move, by the way." - Dave (Alexander England)

12. Dead Snow (2009)

- "I am not a Nazi zombie, I am a Russian!" - Daniel (Martin Starr)

13. Nightmare City (1980)

- "The situation is out of control." - Dean Miller (Hugo Stiglitz)

14. Blood Quantum (2019)

- "We ain't gonna get through this without ammo." - Lysol (Kiowa Gordon)

15. Slither (2006)

- "Did you just call me f**kface?" - Grant Grant (Michael Rooker)

16. Let Sleeping Corpses Lie (1974)

- "I hope I don't become like them." - George (Ray Lovelock)

17. Night of the Comet (1984)

- "If either of you ever picks up a weapon again, I'll beat you to death with my baseball bat." - Reggie (Catherine Mary Stewart)

18. The Serpent and the Rainbow (1988)

- "Don't let them bury me. I'm not dead." - Christophe (Conrad Roberts)

19. Juan of the Dead (2010)

- "Juan of the Dead, we kill your loved ones! How can I help you?" - Juan (Alexis Díaz de Villegas)

20. I Walked With a Zombie (1943)

- "I prayed for you. I prayed that death would free you from your curse." - Wesley Rand (James Ellison)

21. Land of the Dead (2005)

- "Zombies, man. They creep me out." - Cholo (John Leguizamo)

22. 28 Weeks Later (2007)

- "There's no getting out, is there?" - Doyle (Jeremy Renner)

23. Planet Terror (2007)

- "No. You're just making yourself a smaller target. Plus, you look like a pussy." - Cherry Darling (Rose McGowan)

24. Cemetery Man (1994)

- "Timmy, you don't play with your food!" - Helen Robinson (Carrie-Anne Moss)

25. La Horde (The Horde) (2009)

- "You have to face it: we're in deep shit." - Jimenez (Jean-Pierre Martins)

26. Rammbock: Berlin Undead aka Siege of the Dead (2010)

- "Let's just focus on the beer for now." - Michael (Michael Fuith)

27. Zombieland (2009)

- "Nut up or shut up!" - Tallahassee (Woody Harrelson)

28. Night of the Living Dead (1990)

- "I'm sorry, Johnny. I didn't mean to hit you so hard." - Barbara (Patricia Tallman)

29. Dead & Buried (1981)

- "Welcome to Potter's Bluff. A small town with a big secret." - Sheriff Dan Gillis (James Farentino)

30. Wyrmwood: Road of the Dead (2014)

- "We are living in a zombie apocalypse, bro." - Benny (Leon Burchill)

31. The Battery (2012)

- "We are the very, very early wave of whatever is gonna happen." - Ben (Jeremy Gardner)

32. Night of the Creeps (1986)

- "As I live and breathe... the dead!" - Detective Cameron (Tom Atkins)

33. One Cut of the Dead (2017)

- "Keep rolling! This is so much fun!" - Director Higurashi (Takayuki Hamatsu)

34. The Plague of the Zombies (1966)

- "You must believe, my friends. You must believe!" - Squire Hamilton (John Carson)

35. Braindead, aka Dead Alive (1992)

- "Party's over." - Lionel Cosgrove (Timothy Balme)

36. Dawn of the Dead (2004)

- "Zombies, man. They creep me out." - Michael (Jake Weber)

37. Train to Busan (2016)

- "Life is one big karmic circle. You do bad things, and they come back to bite you." - Sang-hwa (Ma Dong-seok)

38. The Beyond (1981)

- "I don't know what's worse: dying or watching someone you love dying." - Liza (Catriona MacColl)

39. [*REC] (2007)

- "I have to pee. I'm going out. I'll be right back." - Ángela Vidal (Manuela Velasco)

40. Pontypool (2008)

- "You do know the actual way to stop it spreading is to kill anyone infected, right?" - Lawrence (Rick Roberts)

41. Demons (1985)

- "What about us? We're trapped in here. And we're fucked!" - Hannah (Fiore Argento)

42. Zombi 2 (1979)

- "We cannot escape from these creatures. They're the living dead." - Dr. David Menard (Richard Johnson)

43. Night of the Living Dead (1968)

- "They're coming to get you, Barbara!" - Johnny (Russell Streiner)

44. Shaun of the Dead (2004)

- "Can I get any of you cunts a drink?" - Shaun (Simon Pegg), mistaking zombies for regular patrons at a pub.

45. Day of the Dead (1985)

- "I'm running this monkey farm now, Frankenstein, and I want to know what the fuck you're doing with my time!" - Captain Rhodes (Joe Pilato)

46. 28 Days Later (2002)

- "Oh great, Valium. Not only will we be able to get to sleep, but if we're attacked in the middle of the night, we won't even care." - Mark (Noah Huntley)

47. Re-Animator (1985)

- "You killed him?" - Dan Cain (Bruce Abbott). "No, I did not." - Herbert West (Jeffrey Combs)

48. Return of the Living Dead (1985)

- "Send... more... paramedics." - Tarman (Allan Trautman), calling for more victims.

49. Dawn of the Dead (1978)

- "When there's no more room in hell, the dead will walk the earth." - Peter (Ken Foree)

50. Dead Set (2008)

- "You're not crazy, Liv. You're post-traumatic, and there's a difference." - Ravi Chakrabarti (Rahul Kohli)

Zombie TV Shows with Quotes

- **iZombie (2015-2019)**
  - "I'm a zombie. It's like the worst zombie-themed superhero ever."
- **Santa Clarita Diet (2017 - 2019)**
  - "So, Mr. Ball Legs... what are we going to do today?"
- **Z Nation (2014 - 2018)**
  - "There's no 'i' in 'zombie.' Oh, wait..."
- **Black Summer (2019)**
  - "Just when you thought running couldn't get any worse..."
- **The Walking Dead (2010 - 2022)**
  - "I hear they're opening a new restaurant. It's called 'The Hungry Dead.' They only serve fresh brains."
- **Fear the Walking Dead (2015 - 2023)**
  - "Why does every apocalypse have to start with someone eating a salad?"
- **The Walking Dead: World Beyond (2020 - 2021)**
  - "When life gives you zombies, make zombie-ade."
- **Daybreak (2019)**
  - "Zombies are like the worst version of an 'eat fresh' diet."
- **In the Flesh (2013 - 2014)**
  - "I'm not dead, I'm just... differently alive."
- **Dead Set (2008)**
  - "Reality TV takes on a whole new meaning when zombies are the stars."
- **Reality Z (2020)**
  - "When life gives you zombies, make a reality show out of it."
- **Kingdom (2019 - 2020)**
  - "Nothing says 'good morning' like waking up to a zombie apocalypse."
- **Day of the Dead (2021)**
  - "When the dead rise, the living better start running."

- **Helix (2014 - 2015)**
  - "It's not a virus, it's a lifestyle choice."
- **Brand New Cherry Flavor (2021)**
  - "Some people want fame. Others just want to survive a zombie apocalypse."
- **Ash Vs. Evil Dead (2015 - 2018)**
  - "Who needs a chainsaw hand when you've got killer one-liners?"
- **Freakish (2016 - 2017)**
  - "High school drama meets zombie mayhem. What could go wrong?"
- **Death Valley (2011)**
  - "The undead aren't the scariest thing in Death Valley. Have you seen the tourists?"
- **All of Us Are Dead (2022)**
  - "Looks like 'Dead: The Musical' has a new cast member."
- **Zomboat! (2019)**
  - "When the zombie apocalypse hits, it's time to set sail."
- **S.O.Z: Soldiers or Zombies (2021)**
  - "War is hell, but add zombies, and it's a whole new level of insanity."
- **Curfew (2019)**
  - "The only thing worse than rush hour traffic? Rush hour traffic during a zombie outbreak."
- **The Returned (2015)**
  - "They're baaack... and they're hungry."
- **Glitch (2015 - 2019)**
  - "When the dead rise, it's time to reevaluate your life choices."
- **The Last of Us (2023)**
  - "In a world overrun by zombies, it's survival of the fittest. And the sneakiest."
- **The Walking Dead: The Ones Who Live (2024)**
  - "Living in a world of the undead isn't easy. But hey, at least

we're alive... for now."

- **Tales of the Walking Dead (2022)**
  - ○ "Who needs a bedtime story when you can have tales of the walking dead?"
- **The Walking Dead: Daryl Dixon (2023)**
  - ○ "Crossbow: Check. Motorcycle: Check. Badass attitude: Double check."

About the Author

Jinx Blade was born on the brink of a post-apocalyptic era and sent back in time to chronicle her tales. With a penchant for the absurdity of end times, Jinx's writing dives headfirst into chaos, showcasing ordinary people navigating through absolute hell with a side of snark and a dash of dark humor.

Inspired by George Romero's "Dawn of the Dead" in high school, Jinx's obsession with zombies never waned. Armed with wit and a love for the undead, she fearlessly blends heart-pounding action with laugh-out-loud moments.

When not conjuring up post-apocalyptic worlds, Jinx indulges in horror movies and perfecting her zombie survival plan (hint: lots of canned beans and a trusty chainsaw).

So get ready for a wild ride through the end of the world with Jinx Blade. Just remember: when zombies attack, laughter might be your best weapon.